The

Bikini

Collective

Book 3: Sea of Gratitude

Kate McMahon

First published by Kate McMahon in 2020
This edition published in 2020 by Kate McMahon

Sea of Gratitude: The Bikini Collective
ISBN: 978-0-6484782-2-5 PRINT
ISBN: 978-0-6484782-3-2 E-BOOK
The Bikini Collective/Kate McMahon

Cover design by Pepita Wilson
Cover surfing photography by richardkotchphotography.com

Kate McMahon has spent the past twenty years surfing waves all over the world, and regularly arriving to events late with her hair dripping wet. After watching many of her friends compete on the world surfing tour, she wondered how she too could combine a career with her true love; her butt still hurts from pinching herself after landing the dream job as editor of *SurfGIRL* magazine in 2001. Since then, Kate has edited various preschool, tween, teen and music magazines and lives just 100 steps from the sand at Narrabeen on Sydney's Northern Beaches, where she gets up to mischief with all of her amazing surfer girlfriends.

www.katemcmahonmyword.com

 facebook.com/katemcmahonmyword

 twitter.com/thekatemcmahon

 instagram.com/thebikinicollectivebook

To the Leilas – my group of female Brazilian friends who've allowed me in as the Latino-like *gringa*. Thank you for the crazy times we've had over many years, I cherish your friendship, cheese balls and you for leading me astray on my first trip to Brazil, where I earned the nickname Kaychee do Rosa (for reasons withheld *wink*).

ACKNOWLEDGEMENT OF COUNTRY
I acknowledge the Traditional Custodians of the Lands on which I write and the beaches that I surf and recognise their continued connection to Land, waters and community. Aboriginal and Torres Strait Islander peoples are the Land's first storytellers. I pay my deepest respect to Elders past, present and future.

#1

Thoughts swirl around Carolyn's head and anxiety tugs at her insides like a brutal rip bank that's draining out with the low tide. This sucks. She doesn't get it; why her? Everything was going sweet. But like always, as soon as she's ruling at life the universe bitch-slaps her back down again.

'Crap.'

Preoccupied by the news she copped only an hour ago, Carolyn spies the wave rising in front of her a little too late. Fumbling to lean onto the rails of her surfboard and pierce it through the water, her lack of timing sees the pitching lip pick her up and throw her backwards with a thud. Not even Mother Nature will give her a break today. Fighting her way through the turbulent whitewater towards the surface feels like a parallel of her life out of the ocean.

When she was a kid she didn't care; she wasn't conditioned to care. Back then she didn't notice that her home was a fraction the size of most of her friends' houses, or that her white bread jam sandwich lunch paled in comparison to their five-food-group spread. She didn't realise how awkward it was for the teacher when the rest of the class made Father's Day craft. But now she cares. She cares heaps.

Taking a freestyle stroke over to her runaway surfboard, she slides back onto the deck, allowing her dark, sea-soaked curls to flop over her face. Indecision tugs her back and forth. Should she paddle out to try again, or retreat to shore, emotionally exhausted? Heading in waveless is a surfer's worst sign of defeat, a feeling that can linger and irk for the entire day.

An opportunity presents itself. It could be judged as a surfing cop-out, but she takes it anyway. A small bump of ocean peels towards her and she bellies onto the whitewater, angling towards the green section of the wave, then springs quickly to her feet. She leans aggressively onto her back foot to slice her fins into the bottom of the wave, then reaches the top, whipping her upper body around to send a rooster tail of water high into the late afternoon air. Since qualifying for the

World Junior Tour this year, the event commentators have commended her power surfing style, bellowing through the speakers their go-to comparison of her 'surfing like a guy'. The benchmark makes her smile, but it makes her best friend Mel Appleby bristle. 'Why is men's surfing setting the standard of what's deemed the best?' Mel argues. 'Who's to say the grace and style of women's surfing shouldn't be measured more highly than a man's guts, gonads or power?'

Carolyn usually just nods. She gets it, she really does. And deep down she's passionate about this feminist stuff too. But she's got way more to keep her mind in turmoil than Mel has. Mel's biggest stress is having to cram for an exam after spending her study time sneaking out the bedroom window of her beachside family home to party without her parents (who are still together, by the way) realising she's gone. In Carolyn's eyes, that scenario is an absolute luxury.

The shore draws nearer as she pumps her board through the final section of the wave and lazily floats over the foam, then crouches down to ride until her fins scrape into the sand of the shallows. Her watch blinks 4:40 pm, giving her just 20 minutes to change out of her springsuit and into her clothes, then hightail it to her part-time job at Pacific Grove's only surf shop, Offshore. The last thing she needs right now is to jeopardise her income. She's managed to save $997 so far this year, but her mum's just asked to borrow $200 of it to make rent this month, and her timing couldn't be worse. What can she do though, say no? *Nah, soz Mum, I don't want to help you pay for the home I live in.*

The thought of her mum tightens a knot in her stomach. She was only nineteen when she found out she was pregnant; just four years older than Carolyn is now. About to go to teacher's college, seeing bands every weekend. She even tried surfing back then, until her life got flipped on its head. Carolyn's been riddled with guilt about it ever since she could comprehend the situation.

She hangs her head for a moment, looking at the frayed laces she just tied when she hears her name being called across the car park.

'Hey!' Her other best friend, Jaspa Ryder, skips over with an almost-new surfboard tucked under her long slender arms. 'You left class early, someone said they saw you in Mr Mackeral's office. Everything okay?'

Carolyn looks up at Jaspa and studies the blonde hair falling down to her waist, her blue eyes free from angst or bitterness. Her hot boyfriend stands by her side, stroking her back. Jaspa's version of okay is so far removed from Carolyn's. She swiftly rises to her feet and shoves a cap over her wet hair. 'Yeah, dude,' she says, eyes downcast, fumbling to slip her arm through her one backpack strap while the broken one flaps about, yet to be repaired. 'It was nothin', he just wanted to check in about the next leg of the tour.'

Jaspa jiggles on the spot, clapping her hands. 'I know, I can't believe we're going to Brazil in three weeks! Mum and Dad said they'll take us to that giant Jesus on the mountain, and to Rio beach which is really famous, and I'm not sure what I'll eat as I'm 100 per cent vegetarian now, and …'

'Yep, I can't believe it either,' Carolyn cuts in, wincing at the double meaning in her words. She leans over and grasps for the skateboard she hid in the bushes, about to make a quick exit to avoid further dialogue, when she feels the weight of someone launching onto her back and loses sight as her cap is pulled over her eyes.

'Hey,' she shouts. 'What the fu–'. A familiar laugh blurts into her ear and she wrestles around to see Mel, teeth gritted in a grin and ready for combat as they fall to the ground.

'Dude,' Carolyn says, dusting off her T-shirt and pushing against her heels to wriggle away from Mel. 'These are my work clothes, ya psycho.'

'Well, that's what you get for skipping class and not

including me in the presumably illegal or at least questionably immoral fun.'

Mel stands and reaches out a hand, which Carolyn dubiously accepts, unsure if it'll result in the old offer-and-retract action. She's surprised when she finds herself being helped to her feet.

Carolyn suspects an ulterior motive. It's not that Mel's incapable of doing nice things, it's just that if you look hard enough you'll usually spot at least a smidgen of a hidden agenda between the courteous cracks. Carolyn studies Mel's smirk and her sharp eyes, which carry so much clarity and courage. She really was hoping she wouldn't see her this afternoon. With Jaspa, you can mask a brave face, gloss over the grit. But Mel, she'll metaphorically wring out your entire body until you cave into the truth. Carolyn decides her best plan of action is to avoid eye contact with Mel for the foreseeable future, at least until she's got herself untangled from this unfolding mess.

'I didn't skip class,' Carolyn says, tucking her surfboard under her arm and placing her front right foot on the skateboard in a goofy stance. 'I was just called into Macca's office about Brazil next month. You know, flights and all that crap.'

Mel's eyes narrow. 'But our flights were booked yonks ago.'

'I know, that's what he was checking. Dude, don't stress. I've gotta bounce. Later.' Carolyn pushes off the car park bitumen to roll onto the smooth surface of the walkway, leaving Mel's obvious suspicion lingering behind her.

#2

Her phone screen lights up the otherwise darkened room, awaking Carolyn with a start. It's a message from Mel.

> *Get your hot ass outta bed, Off The Breakwall has an epic bank, we're picking you up to hit it before school.*

Carolyn groans and pulls the sheets up to her eyes. She's aware that as a surfer she's supposed to embrace the dawny – the early morning rise to paddle out at first light. But, heck, on any given day she'd trade the ideal glass-off you get at a 5 am wake-up call for more time cocooned in her doona. Especially now, as the seasons are starting to shift. The humidity that used to linger into the early hours has been replaced by a bite in the air that allows Carolyn to wear her favourite attire – black skinny jeans and a red and grey flanno shirt – without being soaked in sweat, at least until the full strength of the sun pierces the north coast sky.

So, I can see you've read the message. No backing down now. Get up, we're there in 15.

Jesus, okay, Carolyn thinks. She leans from the bed to fumble for the closest item of clothing on her floor, slipping on a clean pair of boy-leg underwear and track-suit pants featuring a rip-off of the Adidas white stripes on the outer leg. She picks up a plain blue T-shirt, sniffs it, then puts it on, ties a long-sleeved denim shirt around her waist and shoves a cap backwards on her head. She wades through the mess of clothes on her bedroom floor and enters the lounge room with a groan.

Picking up her school bag, she stuffs in a packet of salt and vinegar chips, two mandarins and a full water bottle, then walks over to where her mum is sprawled on the black leather-look lounge that has started to split at the seams.

Urgh, Tanya you're a fricken' train wreck. A cigarette still rests between her mother's fingers, ash spilling over the couch onto the floor, and an empty wine bottle protrudes from under the couch, knocking against Carolyn's foot. She pinches the cigarette butt away from her mum's grip and places it in the ashtray on the coffee table, then smells her fingers in disgust.

'Mum. Mum. TANYA!' She shakes her mum's shoulder. 'Wake the heck up and get into bed, for Christ's sake.'

'Huh? What?' her mum drools, disoriented and licking her dry lips.

Carolyn slings an arm behind her mum's back and helps her upright. 'Go and lay down for a couple of hours and get yourself presentable. You know you're on your final warning at work.'

Sorrow wrinkles Tanya's brow as the shame from last night's slip-up sets in. 'Honey, I'm so sorry. I won't do it again.'

'Mum, don't fire empty words at me.' Carolyn helps Tanya to her feet and watches her shuffle to the darkened bedroom. 'I've heard it all before,' she calls to the closing door.

Carolyn hears the bed squeak under her mum's weight. She takes a moment to clean up the lounge room, then picks up her surfboard and sits on the outside step to wait for Mel and Jaspa.

A thought pops into her head. One that she's tried

to suppress over the years: *Would her mum be this cracked apart if Carolyn's dad had stuck around all those years ago?* Every time Carolyn has probed her mum for more information, Tanya's offered a response riddled with guilt: it was one night, she couldn't remember his full name, and he took off before Carolyn was born, back to somewhere that wasn't Australia. That's all Carolyn knows about that particular branch of her family tree. The only thing is, there are holes in her story. When she was six, Carolyn found a photo of her as a baby being held by a dark-skinned young man with black wavy hair and brown eyes. She'd showed it to her mum, asking *Is this Daddy?* Despite her mum insisting it wasn't, Carolyn still wonders. Every time she catches a look of her coal-like eyes in a mirror, or absently strokes her mocha-toned skin, she wonders. She never saw that photo again.

Seeing headlights approach, Carolyn walks down the driveway towards Cooper's hatchback.

'Yo,' she greets as Jaspa winds down the passenger side window. 'Thanks for the pick-up. No thanks for the wake-up,' she adds, standing on the car's side panel to reach up to the roof racks and secure her board in place.

Mel opens the back door on the far side and wrenches herself up to peer over the car at Carolyn. 'I will accept full credit for your wake-up, and full credit for the sick barrels you're about to be swallowed up by. Now, get in.'

Carolyn flicks her fingers at Mel across the roof of the car then pulls herself into the back seat, only to be tickle-tackled by Mel before she has a chance to put on her seatbelt. 'Hey, ya nutjob,' Carolyn says, trying to catch Mel's hands to prevent further torture. 'I'm still bloody half asleep.'

Jaspa turns from the front seat with a grin. 'How was work last night, was it busy? Did Brooke tell you any more stories?'

'Alright, no and yes,' Carolyn replies, recalling another deep discussion with her boss and ex-professional surfer, Brooke Ray.

When it's quiet at work, instead of getting Carolyn to pretend to be busy, Brooke schools her on surfing history and what it was like living in Pacific Grove back in the day. 'It was super quiet because of the rain, so–'

'Sick! So, what goss did you unearth this time?' Mel cuts in.

'Jesus, girl, I'm getting there.'

Cooper grins at Carolyn in the rear-vision mirror. Being Jaspa's boyfriend and the only one of the four of them with a driver's licence, he's used to being the fourth wheel, with wheels, and playing chauffeur to the three best friends.

'So, yo, get this,' Carolyn begins as Jaspa and Mel look on intently. 'You know how surfer chicks are sometimes called Gidget?'

Jaspa and Mel nod. 'Isn't that just a surf brand?' Jaspa asks.

'Nup,' Carolyn says. 'It's an actual person. Some girl from, like, the freakin' '50s or something, surfed Malibu–'

'What, Malibu where we competed this year?' Jaspa asks.

'Yep, that one.' Carolyn nods. 'Listen. So she hung out in Malibu and got taught to surf, on mals obviously, by a bunch of dudes, then told her dad and he made a film or book or some crap out of it, and the whole thing went mad – like, even here in Australia. Her name's Katy, or something, but she was a short arse so she got called Gidget.'

Jaspa's brow furrows. 'But why – what does that even mean?'

'No way, check her out,' Mel says, holding out her phone. 'It says here her name's Kathy Kohner and the nickname's a mix of 'girl' and 'midget'. That's so cool. That might be my new name for you, Carolyn.'

Carolyn whacks Mel's shoulder. 'Rack off! Half an inch difference does not give you that right.'

'Look how cute she is,' Jaspa says, pinching the phone screen with her fingers to enlarge the photo. 'Swimwear was so awesome back then, so retro.'

The car's tyres crackle over the gravel and stop at the fence. 'We're here,' Cooper says, interrupting their conversation about high-waisted bikinis making a comeback, and Carolyn's insistence that there's no way in heck she's going there.

'Oh yeah, baby!' Mel is the first to spring from the car and see the beach. 'Look at those a-frames of awesome.'

Carolyn climbs out and helps Cooper take the boards down from the roof. In the distance, across a bed of chalky sand spiked with seagrass, lines of swell sweep across the ocean like corrugated iron. They march in from the hazy horizon and bounce against the rock groin to form wave peaks along the 400-metre stretch of beach. The offshore wind fans a spray towards the back of the wave, like a cockatoo's crest that's been soaked by a sprinkler.

'Dudes, you were right. These banks are sickness.' Carolyn wraps a towel around her body and grabs her springsuit from her bag.

'Whoa,' Mel says, pulling her one-millimetre long-sleeved rash vest over her bikinis. 'You're peaking way too early with all that rubber. The air's cooler, but the water's still twenty-three degrees.'

'I'll take my chances, thanks. Being cold sucks.'

'I wonder what Brazil will be like?' Jaspa asks, as they fix their leg-ropes to their ankles and walk across sand that's so clean it squeaks between their toes. 'Water temp wise, I mean.'

Carolyn picks up her pace, breaking into a jog. 'See you out there,' she says, keen to avoid the conversation. 'We've only got two hours before class,' she calls behind her.

As soon as she enters the water her bladder releases and warmth trickles down her leg from beneath the rubber. Carolyn sighs with relief, opens up the shorts of her wetsuit to flush in some water, then hops on her board to paddle out towards an empty left-hander. The sun is beginning to creep over the horizon, sending airbrushed strokes of orange across the sky. Carolyn sits up on her board and waits for her first wave.

Despite the beauty of her surroundings, and the unabashed pleasure of a sport that allows you to piss at the same time, Carolyn feels heavy. Her mind is loaded with worries. In moments of stillness like this, the worries gather together and weigh her down, making it tough to know which one to tackle first.

A bump in the ocean moves towards her, offering her a moment of relief. She takes four hard strokes against the offshore wind and airdrops to face a folding lip. The moment she lands at the base of the wave, she steers her board to slot herself into the barrel and places her weight on her back foot to stall. A wall of water tunnels around her, collecting her thoughts along the way.

In that moment, Carolyn's mind can be nowhere else. Does her stance feel good? Does she need to increase or decrease speed? Will she reach the light of the open air before the wave pinches down on her? These are the only questions in her mind right now. Not, why does her mum drink too much? Why does she look so different to her friends? Does her dad still exist? And does she have the guts to tell her two best friends the truth?

#3

'Girls, Cooper, you're late.' Thomas Sampson turns and taps his watch with the marker he's using to write on the whiteboard as the four of them attempt to sneak into the classroom with dripping wet hair and surf-soaked grins on their faces.

'Soz, Mr Sampson,' Carolyn says, eyes downcast, as she slides into the seat next to Mel.

'Yeah, sorry Thommo,' Mel says, waving a bit of paper in the air. 'We've got a late note from Huey excusing us cos the waves are puuuuuumping,' she adds, singing out the last word in falsetto.

'Mel,' Thomas says, folding his arms to signify annoyance while secretly amused by his student's attempt to use the Surfing God as a truancy scapegoat.

'That's Mr Sampson, and that's your final warning on that. And the excuse of good surf is barely palatable to a classroom full of surfers.'

Carolyn kicks Mel under the desk as Thomas masks a grin and turns back to the whiteboard. 'Dude, one day he'll actually expose his bad side and slap you with suspension.' Carolyn's aware of the resentment peppered through her statement. If it wasn't for the surfing scholarship she'd won, there's no way she could afford to attend the Institute of Sporting Excellence. She'd still be at West Pacific Grove High with all the other neighbourhood kids, where classroom riots and boozing at the bus shelter is the norm. So, in Carolyn's mind, she has to achieve next-level good behaviour compared to everyone else, for fear of losing her privileges and being booted out.

She looks up at Thomas as he scribbles passionately on the whiteboard. This is the man who helped her score the scholarship in the first place. He was an old friend of her boss's. Once a month Brooke runs a community night at the surf shop for local troubled kids. The kids come along and watch surfing videos and play ping-pong so they can forget about home life for a while. That's where Carolyn met Thomas; he volunteers at the community nights.

She was three months into her first year of high school when he suggested she apply for funding to attend the Institute of Sporting Excellence and join the elite surfing program. Brooke had shown him footage of Carolyn surfing, and he was impressed. Surfing, for school? Carolyn couldn't dream up a better scenario. But what did she know about applying for grants?

A lump of emotion clogs Carolyn's throat every time she thinks about how Thomas helped her draft her submission and wrote her a letter of recommendation. Why would someone she barely knows want to help her? Before she knew it, she was facing a panel of people in suits and fumbling through a list of the qualities she could bring to the school. Her guess for what got her over the line? Along with slightly above-average marks in maths, she could be relatable to those minorities who don't fit the stereotypical image of the blonde-haired, blue-eyed surfer girl.

'Righto!' Thomas claps his hands, bringing the class to attention. 'Today's topic for discussion,' he says, pointing to the big, bold text behind him that reads: Surfing in the Olympics and its Impact. He strides to the front of his desk and perches on the edge, his hands resting on the thighs of his Levi bootlegs.

'Jesus, does Thommo never listen?' Mel whispers to

Carolyn. 'I told him to ditch the dad-cut jeans if he wants to score a chick.'

'Shhh,' Carolyn offers through a wide-eyed smirk.

'Mel, Carolyn, let's start the debate with you, seeing as you're both in a chatty mood.'

'Bitch,' Carolyn whispers, jabbing the tip of her elbow into Mel's ribs.

'Surfing will appear in the Olympics for the first time this year,' Thomas says, folding his arms. 'What will this mean for the sport?'

'More crowds and more kooks!' a voice yells from the back of the class.

'Okay, Josh, you're not Mel nor Carolyn, but thank you for your comment. And your reasoning?'

'Cos everyone will see how fun it is and wanna do it.'

'Will they though?' Mel jumps in, turning around in her seat to face Josh. 'Do you *really* think the everyday person who likes to sit on their arse and watch shotput will give a crap about surfing?'

'Yeah, cos it's mad as,' Carolyn offers.

'Sure, *we* know that,' Mel says, keeping her voice loud even though Carolyn is only half a foot away from her. 'But unless you're already a surfer, are you really going to know what the heck is going on? Like, they're used to sports where white lines mean a ball is in or out, or whoever reaches the end of the pool first is the winner.'

'Good point, Mel,' Thomas says. 'So, you're saying the non-surfing spectators will find it hard to understand surfing's scoring system?'

'Totally. Don't you think? They'll get completely lost about why one manoeuvre scores an eight and another gets a three.'

'Unless everyone does airs,' Carolyn adds.

'Well, yeah, that'd be different, I guess. People would go nuts for that.'

'Okay.' Thomas walks over to the whiteboard and begins writing. 'So, the key debating points so far are: potential to trigger more crowds versus the Olympic spectators not fully understanding the scoring system, and that aerial surfing might be the key for mass appeal. What else?'

'Surfing's different from other sports,' Carolyn responds, leaning her elbow on the desk and cradling her head in her hand, her wet ringlets falling between her fingers. 'Like, we don't freakin' do it to stay fit. We wake up, we wanna surf. We're in school, we can't wait to finish so we can surf. We go to bed, we dream about surfing. We have a crap life, but at least we've got surfing.' She shrugs. 'But maybe that is what'll rope in the kooks. Like, the message that you don't have to have an expensive gym or club membership. You just grab an old dunger from the hard rubbish and you can surf for free. Yeah, I reckon the freedom is what's going to sell surfing.'

Mel pushes on the desk to lean back in her chair with a scoff. 'Ah, the irony right there. Freedom being used to *sell* surfing.'

Carolyn stares ahead and allows her mind to wander. She cringes to think what her life would be like without surfing. It's the place she escapes to when her mum brings home a new boyfriend who she claims is 'the one this time', who either has zero idea of how to interact with a teenager so simply grunts hello, tries too hard to interact and won't shut up, or whose breath stinks of dog crap. In the ocean, every surfer's equal: no one can see the house you live in or the car you drive, or know you've had pizza for dinner five nights in a row. And whether you're deemed beautiful or not won't make it any easier to paddle into waves. All that matters is you, your surfboard and the sea.

'You coming or what?' Mel's out of her seat, her pineapple-print backpack slung over one shoulder, as the rest of the students exit the classroom.

'Huh? Oh, yep,' Carolyn says, trying to wedge her

pen and phone into the tight pocket of her skinny jeans. She follows Mel and Jaspa out into the courtyard so they can walk together to their Spanish class.

'Oh, Carolyn,' says a voice from behind.

'Yeah?' she replies, turning back to see Thomas in the classroom doorway, his arm propping the door open. 'Whaddup, Mr Sampson?'

'I just wanted to say I'm really sorry to hear about your scholarship. Let me know if there's anything I can do to help.'

'Uh huh,' Carolyn mumbles, turning quickly and keeping her eyes down.

'No, no, no, no, no, hold up,' Mel says, launching for Carolyn's elbow before she can quicken her pace. 'What the heck did Thommo mean by that?'

Carolyn yanks her arm out of Mel's grip.

'Don't worry about it, it's nothing to do with you.'

'Of course it's to do with me, what's this crap about your scholarship? Spill.'

'Look, Mel, you can't fix everything, ya know.'

'Carolyn,' Jaspa says, calmly reaching out to touch her shoulder. 'We're your best friends. What's going on?'

'You guys don't know what it's like, okay? Stop pretending we're on the same playing field. We're not, you got it? We. Are. Not. And we never will be.' Carolyn darts quickly from the courtyard across the oval towards the car park. She can feel a ball of anxiety growing inside her chest as she attempts to outpace her friends, feeling more distanced from them than ever before.

#4

'Jesus, wait up,' Mel calls out breathlessly as Carolyn runs to the main road and sticks out her thumb to try and hitch a ride. 'You're being ridiculous.'

'Oh, am I?' Carolyn stops short and turns to face them, using her forearm to wipe the wetness from her face. 'You guys get to go off to Brazil while I'll be stuck in Pacific Grove hell, tending to my dysfunctional mum and whatever clown she decides to bring home this month. But sure, I'm being ridiculous.'

'What … what are you talking about? You're coming to Brazil too,' Jaspa says.

'Nope. No I ain't.'

'But our flights are booked, you said so yourself?'

'They were booked, and now they're not. Well, mine at least.'

Mel screws up her face. 'What? This makes no sense.'

'You getting in?' asks a scruffy-haired guy from the passenger side of the P-plated hatchback that's just stopped on the side of the road.

'Yep,' Carolyn says, walking over and reaching for the back door.

'No she isn't, rack off,' Mel says, grabbing both of Carolyn's wrists and dragging her away from the car.

'Let me go, you freakin' psycho,' Carolyn says, trying to wriggle out of Mel's grip.

'Later, weirdos,' says the guy as the car screeches off, leaving the girls engulfed in a cloud of dust and gravel.

'This makes no sense,' Mel repeats. 'What the heck is going on?'

Carolyn's chest expands as she sucks in as much air as she can, then expels it just as quickly. 'It actually makes perfect sense. Welcome to my life. My scholarship funds aren't enough for me to finish the tour.'

'Oh, man, no, that sucks.' Mel sits down on the curb and waves away the dust. 'And you only just found out?'

'Yesterday,' Carolyn says, kicking at the gravel. 'Something about the American dollar being strong or some crap. Anyway, I don't have enough left for Brazil let alone the rest of the tour. And losing in the early rounds of the last few comps hasn't helped the prize money sitch.'

Mel hangs her head between her knees while Carolyn and Jaspa remain standing, silent, their thoughts weighing them down like a ball of whitewater pinning them against the sand.

The school bell rings in the distance.

'Well, we missed Spanish,' Jaspa says quietly.

'*Si,*' whispers Mel. '*Pero tenemos cosas más importantes que hacer.*'

'Freakin' showoff,' Carolyn scoffs. 'I still suck at Spanish.'

Mel springs to her feet. 'Well,' she says, wrapping an arm around Carolyn's shoulder and coaxing her back towards the school, apparently hoping her enthusiasm is contagious. 'You'd better start brushing up on your Portuguese for Brazil.'

'Dude, I'm not going, don't you get it?' Carolyn pulls away from Mel's touch.

'Yeah, but–' Mel begins, but Carolyn raises her hand to cut her off.

'No, Mel. I've spent my life dealing in disappointment, this is nothin' new to me. I keep my expectations low, so I've got less distance to crash on my arse.'

'I could ask Mum for the money,' Jaspa says, slipping out of her paisley kimono throw and stuffing it into her hessian shoulder bag.

'No,' Carolyn says quickly. 'No way, it's too much. I'm not a charity case.'

'How much are we talking?' Mel asks.

'Over three thousand for Brazil alone. Three thousand, five hundred and fifty, to be exact.'

'Crap.'

'Yep.'

As they wander across the oval and head towards H block, already late for maths, Carolyn wonders what this means for school. Will she be booted out? They're hardly going to want to teach someone who can't afford to put the skills into practice. Should she ask her boss for a pay rise? But she already received a bonus last month, when her mum defaulted on the rent. What if she just forgets this life completely and starts a new one? Stuffs everything into her backpack, slings her board into her travel bag and hitches down to Sydney, or even across to WA. Tempting, but could she really leave her mum behind like that?

'What about a Kickstarter campaign?' Jaspa offers as they walk across the courtyard, the full strength of the autumn sun beaming onto their backs.

'No, no way, I said no charity.'

Mel stops Carolyn at the door of the classroom.

'What about a different kind of charity, where people actually *get* something from it?' Mel asks.

'Dude, I don't think your mum could make that many jelly cakes even if she tried.' Carolyn waves her hand in annoyance, keen to dismiss any more ideas. 'Can you just forget about it? I've accepted it, you should too.' She walks through the door, mumbling an apology to the teacher for being late, and sits next to the school's tennis champion Jason Nyall to avoid her friends bugging her further.

Mel bends close to Carolyn's ear as she passes. 'No. I will not forget about it, nor will I accept it.'

As Mel walks away, Jason leans over. 'What's that all about?'

'That,' Carolyn says, 'is delusion.'

#5

The doorbell rings. Carolyn glances up from her surfing magazine to see two girls walk through into the shop and make a beeline for the bikini bargain bin. Their hair is straight and immaculately brushed. There's no way hair can reach that level of perfection of its own accord. Nope, a straightener plus something that comes from a bottle with the promise of gloss or frizz-free or nourishment is definitely involved. Along with time to actually give a crap about such tasks.

Carolyn absently tugs at one of the curls that springs from just below her ear. 'You right?' she asks the girls as they giggle and hold swimwear against their bodies, snapping selfies to assess which items are worth trying on.

'Yeah,' replies the blonder one of the two, with an

attitude-ridden inflection, a duck-lipped pout and a bat of her eyelash extensions.

Carolyn stares a little too long, mesmerised by the lengths they've gone to in order to look like someone other than themselves. The darker-haired girl sneers at Carolyn and raises her brows, which look like they're etched on with Sharpie, then pulls her friend away to the change room with a giggle. Not a friendly giggle; one that's definitely at someone else's expense. Being the only other person in the room, Carolyn doesn't need to tap into her mathematical prowess to work out that equation.

They'll probably steal stuff, Carolyn concludes. Usually she would care. She likes her boss and doesn't want her being ripped off. But today she's exhausted. It's like the last bit of rug holding up a pile of disappointment has been yanked out from under her, and she's using all of her energy to avoid suffocation.

'Where's Stuart?' says a voice at the counter. It's the girls again. So that's why they were unimpressed when they first came in; they were disappointed to see Carolyn managing the store instead of her scruffy-haired, tight-abbed workmate.

'He's away,' Carolyn says dryly, not willing to offer more than that.

'No kidding, genius.' The girls walk away. 'You know, you shouldn't stare so much. It's a bit, like, lezzo.'

Carolyn wishes Mel was here to deliver the ultimate scathing comeback. Unable to think of anything, she swoops up a middle finger and hopes it's not caught on security camera. It's not like she can afford to lose her job.

She looks back down at the 2002 edition of *Surf-GiRL*. Her boss has a mind-blowing collection of magazines that the staff are free to flick through during quiet periods. Brooke doesn't mind if they're sitting around while it's quiet, as long as they're learning about surfing history.

A page catches her eye. It shows a picture of a young woman with a crooked-toothed grin, black hair cut into an untidy bob and a face dotted with freckles. Big, bold font beside the picture blares: 'Am I Not Pretty Enough?' Carolyn's heart sinks when she reads that the woman is Penny Menthol, the 1999 World Champion surfer who had to quit the tour two years later because she couldn't find a sponsor.

According to the article, she'd sold her car, furniture and practically everything she owned to travel on the tour, qualify, then win the world title in her rookie year, but her winnings from the event didn't cover the ongoing cost of travelling. 'You're not the right fit for our brand' is the excuse Penny was given over and over when on the hunt for sponsorship. It's not difficult for Carolyn to join the dots; the rest of the magazine is filled with gorgeous surf-lifestyle models who were being paid six figures even though they could barely turn a surfboard.

Carolyn gets it; marketability and all that. The pretty girls in the posters are the ones who sell bikinis. But that means one of the best surfers in the world had to stop, all because of money, and all because of her appearance. Carolyn sighs and reads on. Penny argues that there should be a balance of both, which gets Carolyn thinking. It's so true. If all young girls see is a beautiful, slim, perfect-skinned girl in the surfwear advertisements, then that's what the sport will attract – more of the same, while other girls will feel hesitant to try surfing for fear of not fitting in. But if people like Penny got to celebrate who they are and how they look in advertisements, then other girls would also feel like they belong. The more diversity is represented, the more difference it attracts. Carolyn realises that this is exactly the argument she put forward to help her get a place in her school.

She taps her phone screen to bring up The Bikini Collective page. This is the perfect message to post on the page she and her friends started. But she hesitates, her thumbs poised above the screen, not knowing where to start and feeling vulnerable about showing her emotions. Instead, she makes a metal note to tell Jaspa, who will convey the message much more eloquently than she can.

On the final page of the story, there's a small photo of Penny standing behind a cafe counter using the steam wand to heat up a jug of milk. A part-filled cup of syrupy coffee sits in front of her. The caption says that this is now Penny's full-time job, and that her competitive surfing dream is over.

Carolyn's chest tightens, scared she's staring into the face of her future. But is this world really ready to allow the shift necessary for her to find a place in it? Her heart says yes, but her head counters it with a big, fat nup.

#6

'What, are you stalking me now?' Carolyn turns from locking up the surf shop to see Mel and Jaspa standing behind her on the sidewalk, grinning broadly. 'I've just finished work. I'm really not in the mood for this, ya know.'

Mel forms her hands into a prayer position. 'We're not here to punish, I promise. I see you've got your board. Do you have any spare clothes?'

'Yeah,' Carolyn says, holding up her backpack. 'Why?'

'We're kidnapping you to Bonita Shores for the weekend. We can all stay at Jaspa's.'

'Mum's picking us up in ten minutes,' Jaspa says, reaching out for Carolyn's surfboard so she can put her keys into her backpack. 'She's just at the shops.'

'Look,' Carolyn protests, 'I fully appreciate it, but I'm just crappy company right now.'

'That may well be,' Mel says, folding her arms. 'But Paradise Point is going to be glassy goodness this weekend.'

'Plus, we have a proposal we think you're gonna love,' Jaspa adds, jiggling on the spot.

'Okay,' Carolyn sighs. 'But only if your mum promises to make that cheesy potato bake thingy.'

'We're one step ahead of you,' Jaspa giggles. 'Mum's just been shopping for all your favourite snacks. Here she is now.'

A black four-wheel drive pulls up to a loading zone with its hazard lights blinking. Jaspa's mum beeps the horn, and as Carolyn sees Ellen waving from the front seat her eyes well up, catching her completely off-guard. As much as she tries to keep people at bay, Jaspa's mum always manages to break down her emotional brick wall with a soft kindness that Carolyn's not used to at home.

'Shall we?' Mel says, taking Carolyn's board and putting it in the back, then opening the car door and ushering Carolyn inside.

'Hi Mrs Ryder,' Carolyn says, yanking herself up into the back seat as Mel shuffles in next to her. 'Thanks for the invite to stay.'

'No problem. Here, girls,' Ellen says, handing out three protein bars. 'This will see you over until dinner.'

'Thanks Mrs Ryder,' Carolyn says. 'So, what's this master proposal, then?' Carolyn asks Mel through mouthfuls of the chewy snack.

'Well, I was going to wait until we're on the main highway so you can't escape. Promise not to bail out of this moving vehicle?'

'Nope, I can't promise nothin', but try me.'

Jaspa turns from the front seat, nibbling away at the chocolate coating on the protein bar, excited to tell Carolyn about their idea.

'Mrs Ryder, can you please put the child lock on Carolyn's door?' Mel jokes. 'Okay, so, we were thinking: a Bikini Collective day on–'

'But we do those all the time, and we don't charge money,' Carolyn cuts in. Carolyn loves the surf days they hold every few months. They started the Bikini Collective to support other girls getting into surfing, and to give them a platform to connect with each other and discuss their achievements and fears, and it's made a huge impact on the number of girls showing interest in the sport. They even held a Bikini Collective event while they were in California. But this is something they donate their time to – there's no money involved. Why would Mel and Jaspa think this could get Carolyn to Brazil?

'If you allow me to finish, I was going to say, *on steroids*. Sure, we run a girls' surf day, but it'll be so much more than that, and that's why we can charge for it.'

Carolyn sighs. 'Okay, I'm listening.'

Jaspa turns down the car stereo then swivels around in the passenger seat. 'We don't have all the details figured out yet, but Mum and Dad suggested a few things,' she says, smiling at Ellen. 'An auction of cool stuff donated from the area. Mum said she could help get travel vouchers, beauty packs, homewares and stuff from her clients. And Dad has arranged for us to hold it at the surf club.'

'Yep, and that's not all,' Mel says as Carolyn tries to mask the enthusiasm she's starting to feel. 'Trudy Hardwick is going to donate the board she won her third world title on,' Mel blurts.

'What? No way!'

'Yeah way. And that ain't all. Your boss is donating some surf stuff, too.'

'Whoa, dudes, I can't believe you've done all of this in a day. Thank you.' Carolyn flops her head against the back seat, then turns to look at Mel. 'Really, thanks.' She's still doubtful this will be enough for her to finish the tour, but all these people are going out of their way to help her. The least she can do is be grateful.

As they drive up main street and turn onto Ocean View Avenue and into Jaspa's driveway, the girls peer out of the window and look at each other in excitement.

'Chicks, shall we?' Mel asks, nodding towards the beach.

'Mum, is it okay if we have a sneaky surf before dinner?'

'Yes love. Don't worry about the groceries, I'll get Dad to help. Off you go.'

'Cheers, Mrs Ryder, you're awesome,' says Carolyn, quickly changing into her springsuit and watching from the driveway as a wave swoops around the headland and hits the suck-rock to push a perfectly-formed right-hander towards the beach. The wall of whitewater plays its role, giving power to the wave, but without hindering the beauty of its open face. Carolyn stands transfixed, mesmerised by the symbolism of a wave this perfect sitting outside Jaspa's house. Her perfect house, with her perfect parents, where there's always delicious food on the table and a warm hug before bed. Carolyn's closest home break is an unpredictable shore dump, with a relentless rip and only a one-hour window each day when it could be considered as good.

'C'mon, c'mon,' Mel says, tapping her leg-rope against her surfboard. 'Tyler and Cooper just paddled in, so we've got the Point all to ourselves.'

They squeak across the sand, which is cooling with every minute of the sun's descent. 'Perhaps we should just paddle out from here?' Jaspa says as they reach the water's edge.

'Yeah,' Mel agrees. 'By the time we clamber over the rocks to the top of the Point, it'll be snack o'clock for the sharkies.'

'Dude,' Carolyn says, flicking Mel with her hand. 'Don't say that. Jesus.' The thought of sharks gives Carolyn the creeps. She's only seen one once, on a sunny day last October when she was standing on the sand with Mel and Jaspa. They were about to paddle out when they spotted the silhouette of a two-metre shark cruising through the back of a breaking wave. Mel was still keen to surf, but there was no fricken' way Carolyn and Jaspa were going out, so they got changed and went for ice-cream instead. Carolyn tries not to think about the fact that they're about to enter the ocean as the sun disappears. 'There's some fun little rollers here off the end anyway, so let's hit it. Quickly,' she says.

Carolyn takes a run-up and bellies her board into the ocean, keeping her momentum gliding with a succession of quick paddle strokes to push her into position. Even though they're sitting at the tail end of the rides, it's still longer than the average wave and twice as fun. She positions herself to be carried by a ball of whitewater, then pops to her feet to carve into the blue blanket of ocean. As dusk settles in, the ocean breeze drops and it's only her movement that alters the wave's appearance; spray from her goofy-footed off-the-top attack, a carved line from her rebound cutback. It's like she's drawing her very own storyboard. If only she could have that much control of her life's back on land.

#7

Carolyn is floored by how smoothly the Bikini Collective day comes together, and at how many people are willing to get involved. Before she knows it, she finds herself at the event, struggling to believe that Party Wave are standing right in front of her, setting up to play at *her* fundraiser. She's loved them ever since they won the New South Wales School Rox band competition and went on to come third in the national title. With their signature skinny-jeaned, chequered-shirted look, she could almost be their fifth member.

The lead singer and guitarist Jay Rose hoists his leg onto an amplifier to tune his mustard-coloured Les Paul. As he twangs the bottom E string and adjusts it to key, he launches into a garage punk-soaked solo, his fingers held in a power chord position, sliding up and down the neck of the guitar as his other hand smashes a plectrum against the bottom three strings in a succession of fast downward strokes.

'Isn't this mad, can you believe it?' Mel says as she sidles up beside Carolyn, rubbing a towel over her wet hair with one hand and jabbing Carolyn in the ribs with the other.

'It's next-level mad. How did Jaspa get them to agree to play in the first place?'

'She asked Thommo to help,' Mel says, nodding at Thomas Sampson, who's on the beach helping bring up the softboards from the Bikini Collective girls' surf lesson. 'He used to do boardriders with the drummer's dad.'

'Man, what a good dude,' Carolyn says. 'I guess we should go and help him bring everything in.'

'Nah, he's got it under control. We need to go and help Jazz and Mrs Ryder with the auction stuff.'

Carolyn greets the Party Wave band members with a nervous nod as she walks inside across the stage and down the three steps onto the dance floor.

'Goodie, you're here!' Jaspa skips over to greet them, her skyscraper legs clumsily out of rhythm beneath her denim miniskirt. 'Come and see what we've done.'

Carolyn follows Jaspa to a long table that features a selection of auction items. Above each item is a sign detailing what it is. Under that is a stack of pages where people can write their name, a price and their contact details. 'What's this?' Carolyn asks, pointing to one of the pages.

'Dad suggested we do this for some of the items. It's a silent auction, so people just write down their bids and the highest one at the end of the night gets it.'

'Check out this one,' Mel says, from the other end of the table. 'This two-night trip to Sydney for four people is currently only going for two hundred bucks. Let's all chuck in so we can surf and then party in Manly. Carn!'

'If I could afford that, I wouldn't need to do this in the first place,' Carolyn says.

'Oh yeah, true dat.'

'So,' Jaspa continues, 'the three big items – Trudy's surfboard, the Eco Valley pamper package, and the five-hundred-dollar surf pack from your boss – are being auctioned off live, by Dad. He reckons he'll be able to coax the crowd into spending heaps.'

'Man, this is so sick, thanks guys,' Carolyn says as Mel and Jaspa embrace her. 'I just can't even deal that all this stuff is for me.'

'Almost ready, girls?' says a voice from behind them.

'Mr Ryder, you are looking smokin',' Mel tells

Jaspa's dad, who's wearing an outfit that's way too cool for an adult.

'See, I told you Tyler's hat would suit you,' Jaspa says, leaning on her dad's shoulder and tipping the brim of the beige fedora. 'You look amazing.'

'Well, I get my style tips from you girls. Okay, Carolyn,' he says, placing a hand softly on her back. 'You come up the front with me.'

'Oh, man, do I have to? I'd rather stay with the girls,' Carolyn says, slumping her shoulders in an attempt to shrink away.

'Yes, yes, you have to, Carolyn. This is your chance to play the crowd. Remember what I told you, puppy dog those baby browns,' Mel says, looking up with widened eyes and a wrinkled brow.

'You know I can't do that. I don't want no charity, remember?'

'It's fine,' says Mr Ryder. 'You can just stand next to me, you don't have to say anything. Jaspa, can you ask the club to turn down the music please?'

Carolyn's stomach does a backflip as she follows Mr Ryder up the stairs and onto the stage to greet the growing crowd. 'Can I have your attention please?' Jaspa's dad says into the microphone. Carolyn gulps. 'Can I have your attention please?' he repeats loudly. 'Welcome to the Bikini Collective fundraiser. This event is being held to allow our little ripper, Carolyn Fitzgerald, to get to Brazil and hopefully finish off this year's World Junior Tour. Carolyn,' he says, smiling down at her, 'we couldn't be happier to be able to help you on this incredible journey. Your surfing talent should take all the credit; we're just here to make things a little easier for you.'

A tear threatens to fall down Carolyn's cheek, but she manages to block it with an over exaggerated nose wipe, and offers Anthony a nervous smile.

'Thanks to all you grom girls who took part in this morning's surf session. Carolyn, Mel and Jaspa have worked hard on creating the Bikini Collective tribe, so let's give them a quick clap – just one; we don't want to be here all night!'

Carolyn laughs as she watches the crowd below her mimic Mr Ryder as he widens his arms and brings his hands together with one loud bang.

'So far,' Mr Ryder says, leaning back to the microphone, 'we've managed to raise $800 on entry tickets and $1,100 – is that right love?' he asks Ellen over the crowd, who nods her head. 'Yep, 1,100 big ones on the silent auction. Thanks so much for your generosity. Okay, let's do this.'

Carolyn fiddles with the corner of her shirt during the auction, trying to keep her mind from wandering and doing the maths. Anthony concludes the bid for the pamper day spa experience at $300, and the surf pack goes for just under its worth at $450. Jaspa walks up to the stage carrying Trudy's board and hands it to Anthony.

'Thanks, button,' Anthony whispers. 'Okay, ladies and gentlemen, this is the moment we've all been waiting for. Drumroll, please,' he says, turning back to the band who stand with their instruments poised, ready to play as soon as the auction's over. The drummer rapid-fires his sticks over the snare, and a succession of hoots can be heard from the crowd.

'Okay, can I have some quiet now please? In my hand, I have three-time world champion Trudy Hard-wick's surfboard, the very one she won this year's Gold Coast Pro event on in February. She sends her apologies that she can't be here to hand this over in person. But given she's in the Maldives, we don't blame her. Okay, can I have an opening bid of over $400 please?'

'$450!' yells a man from the audience.

'$485!' says another.

'C'mon,' Anthony says, 'I think we can do a little better than that.'

'$550!'

'That's more like it.'

'$575!'

'Okay, I'm only accepting increments of over $50 from now on.'

Carolyn keeps her head down but peers out from beneath her curls. Why is everyone being so nice to her? Why have they pushed aside whatever daily problems they have to help solve hers? She feels so exposed up there on the stage, like she's been stripped naked and all her issues are written over her bare body in black marker: Poor. Fatherless. Ugly. Dysfunctional mother. Her temperature rises, and sweat starts to bead on her forehead. Just as she considers bolting, she spies Mel and Jaspa at the front of the crowd, beaming, and Anthony places a hand lightly on her back.

The bidding continues. '$650!'

'$700!'

'$750!'

After a moment of silence, Anthony says: 'Can I get $800? Anybody, $800? This is your last chance to own a bit of surfing history. Imagine if Trudy wins her fourth world title this year. That would mean this very board contributed to that victory. So, I'll ask one more time, can I have $800. No? Okay then–'

'$800!' yells a woman.

'Sold for $800 to the lovely lady at the back.'

Carolyn peers over the crowd to see Ellen's beaming face.

'Who just so happens to be the most beautiful woman here today,' Anthony says, 'and my wife. Thanks very much everyone, we really appreciate your support. Carolyn, the Bonita Shores and Pacific Grove community wish you all the very best. Go and rip it up, girl! Everyone stick around to hear some amazing music from Party Wave.'

The band launches straight into their hit single 'Frothin'', and kids go into a frenzy, banging their heads and pulling out their best air guitar.

Carolyn loosens her chest with a massive sigh and walks over to Mel and Jaspa.

'We did it!' Jaspa claps. 'Did we raise enough for Brazil?'

'Yep, just about,' Carolyn says, looking up at Jaspa, who wraps her arms around Carolyn and almost suffocates her with an embrace. 'I'm only a little short, which I think I can make up with my next couple of pays. I can't believe your mum bought that board. I feel super weird taking her cash.'

'Don't be silly,' Jaspa says, releasing Carolyn. 'Mum had her eye on that board for Dad's room the moment she saw it.'

'Ah, the ol' dude den. Taking its rightful place next to the collection of kooky caps,' Mel laughs, referring to

Anthony's obsession with American baseball memorabilia.

'Still feels weird.'

'Carolyn.' She stiffens as Jaspa rests a hand on her shoulder. 'Sometimes you just have to say "yes, thank you" when someone wants to do something nice for you. It's the greatest gift you can give in return.'

Carolyn looks up at Jaspa and offers an awkward grin. She's sure Penny Menthol would've done anything to have the support that she has now. She slowly nods her head and releases a sigh. 'Yes, thank you.'

#8

Carolyn runs up the stairs to her unit, her backpack hoisted over one shoulder and her surfboard held above her head as a shelter from the rain. The jolt back to reality is harsh. She stayed the weekend at Jaspa's so her folks could help with the logistics of re-organising her trip to Brazil, and to revel in an endless supply of home-cooked food. In among dipping tortilla chips into a dinner-sized bowl of guacamole, and catching the crumbs from Ellen's melting moment biscuits, Anthony drafted her itinerary.

For Friday, Saturday and Sunday nights, Carolyn slept on the trundle bed in Jaspa's room, while Jaspa and Mel shared the queen bed. She would never get sick of the view from Jaspa's balcony, sweeping from Paradise Point all the way up to the North Bonita headland. At night, instead of falling asleep to the sound of kids breaking bottles or couples screaming at each other from the next block, she was soothed by a gentle 'goodnight, girls' from Jaspa's parents and the sound of whitewater crashing down and then receding back over the rocks and sand that line the shore, the volume only adjusting according to the height of the tide. Perhaps that's why Jaspa is such a calm person, Carolyn realises. There's not much there to get angry about.

Carolyn went straight to school from Jaspa's on Monday, enjoying the luxury of travelling in a warm, dry car as they took turns choosing songs through Spotify, Carolyn's continuous spruiking of Aussie hip-hop going entirely unappreciated.

By contrast, the ten-minute walk from the bus stop this afternoon has left her saturated and cold from the rain. Relief overwhelms her as she finally reaches the front door. The key resists against the lock and Carolyn cups one hand over the other to force the key in, then wiggles it around until the latch eventually releases.

The damp smell is immediately apparent, and the carpet just inside the door squelches under Carolyn's feet. 'Jesus,' she belts out, frustrated that the damn leak is still there. On the bright side, it means there's no point drying her surfboard so she allows it to drop to the floor and walks to her bedroom. Her doona is still in the crumpled mess she'd left it in on Friday morning after frantically packing for the weekend at Jaspa's and trying to decide what to take to wear. It was always going to be jeans and a tee, but it's the subtleties that matter. Black, grey or indigo denim? Rips or no rips? Baggy T-shirt or tightly fitted? While she's resigned to getting her clothes from Target or Jay Jays, she won't let her mum skimp on shoes. No way. Black and white Converse hi-tops. They completely define her, help her to feel less of an outcast, but she's dreading the day they start to wear beyond repair.

She unzips her backpack, takes out her clothes and shoves them into the remaining space in her laundry basket. Her wetsuit is still damp. She takes a sniff and recoils at the faint smell of urine. She walks to the bathroom and blasts it with warm water, then hurls it over the rusting shower curtain rod. It drips over her body as she removes her clothes and steps into the shower, jiggling on the spot as she waits for the water to warm up. Her skin prickles as she relaxes under the heat, increasing the temperature in increments as her body adjusts. Carolyn has eight minutes until the hot water runs out. These moments are a luxury to her; it feels like the world almost stops spinning. If thoughts scurry into her head, fine; if they don't, also fine. All that matters are the droplets pelting against her face, massaging her temples and the back of her neck.

A creeping temperature drop warns her of the impending cold burst, so she turns off the taps. The bathroom tiles have cooled, and Carolyn curses under her breath as she realises she forgot to bring the bath mat in from the washing line. The fact that you can feel a sense of luxury with the little things is never lost on Carolyn: a bath mat to warm your feet, food in the fridge when you have an unexpected burst of hunger, discovering a spare block of surfboard wax in your bag when you were about to paddle out waxless.

Memories of the weekend prompt an inward grin as she slips into her tracksuit pants and a long-sleeved jersey. A week ago, she'd resigned herself to the fact that she'd be waving Jaspa and Mel goodbye from the tarmac as they headed for Brazil. Now, she can allow herself to get excited once again. It's a push and pull ritual of permission she's placed upon herself ever since realising what disappointment feels like.

As she heads to the kitchen to see what she can find in the fridge to get creative with, something on the dining table catches her eye. She walks over, avoiding the side of the table that's starting to delaminate, so it doesn't catch on her trackies. A small square envelope with a border of blue, white and red has her name and address scrawled on the front. Usually, the only mail Carolyn gets is from her grandma on her birthday and at Christmas if she's not coming down in person from Rockhampton. Her wages are paid in cash, and everything else is online. So, who's this from?

Above her name it says 'par avion/air mail'. In the top right-hand corner there's a stamp with an illustration of a colourful bird with a big beak – a toucan, she thinks. The Fruitloops bird. Across the envelope are a bunch of official-looking stamps that are smudged from the rain and illegible. Carolyn drops it on the table and goes back to the fridge. It's probably just junk mail, one of those annoying marketing campaigns. But then, why is it addressed to her and not her mum?

The contents of the fridge are bleak: half a loaf of white bread, one overripe tomato, a jar of peanut butter and a smear of avocado still left in the skin. She collects them in her arms and places them on the kitchen bench. With her sandwich snack made, she sits at the table and takes a bite. It's nowhere near as bad as she expected it to be. The peanut butter gives the avocado an almost satay flavour. This is definitely another win for today.

She picks up the envelope again, the tomato juice on her hands creating an instant stain to the paper. The spot for the sender's information is blank. *Yep, this is definitely junk mail,* Carolyn thinks. She uses her fore-finger to rip open the top, pulls out a thin piece of paper and unfolds it. There's a yellow strip with 'Western Union Money Order' in black text. In the middle it states 'three thousand, five hundred and fifty' and next to that is '$3550' and then 'Payable to Carolyn Fitzgerald'. Wait. It's impossible that this is one of those fake cheque campaigns. Is this some kind of sick joke? Because before the fundraiser this weekend gone, this was the *exact* amount of money Carolyn needed to go to Brazil.

#9

'I told you, I have no freakin' idea.' Carolyn walks up Bonita Beach with Jaspa and Mel. This will be their last surf in Australia before they fly out to Brazil that night. The swell has dropped and a northerly sea breeze is ripping into the Point, so they've decided to pack up their regular boards for the trip and borrow playful boards from the Ryders' vast collection to go up to the northern headland. Jaspa has her favourite retro board, which she calls Dotty due to its pattern of polka dots. Mel chose Anthony's banged-up single fin, and Carolyn grabbed a seven-foot mini mal which she's struggling to carry under her arm.

'But the money was legit?' Mel asks, not willing to let this go.

'Yeah, I took it to the bank and they put the money into my account.'

'Far out,' Jaspa says, shaking her head, wide-eyed. 'This is like a movie. Did you ask your mum if she knows anything?'

'Uh huh. She was super weird, but then again, she's always a bit weird. She said it's probably from Mr Sampson or my boss. But it's not, I asked them.'

'That I could buy,' Mel says, scratching her nose and trying not to smudge her zinc. 'But the whole airmail thing is what's got me fascinated.'

'And the fact that it was the exact amount of money you needed to get to Brazil,' Jaspa adds.

The reality of the situation has barely sunk in for Carolyn. She's both completely stoked and completely freaked out. Someone knows her name, knows where she lives and knows that she needed exactly three thousand five hundred and fifty dollars. 'Maybe the airmail thing was just to throw me, maybe they hand delivered it, or sent it from within Australia. I dunno. My head's been exploding with theories. To be honest, I'm just stoked that I can now do most of the main comps this year.' It's difficult for Carolyn to accept this gift guilt-free, especially when her mum seems to be locked in a constant struggle with money. Carolyn can't help but count up the empty cigarette packets and wine bottles in their household rubbish every week. She wants permission to be selfish for a change.

Jaspa places her arm around Carolyn's shoulders and jolts her out of her thoughts. 'You deserve this, Carolyn,' she says. 'And we couldn't imagine doing the tour without you.'

'Well, well,' Mel interrupts. 'Looks like we're being blessed by a fun little send-off session.'

As they reach the shoreline of the surf spot affectionately known as Northies, they're greeted with a rolling left-hander breaking from the rocks all the way to the shore. The shallow sandbank creates a crystal-clear blanket of aqua blue water that sparkles under the mid-morning sun.

'That's a mad little runner,' Carolyn says, placing the mini mal on the sand and attaching the leg-rope to her ankle. She watches Mel do a succession of squats. 'Hey, can you knock out ten of those for me please?'

Mel pauses mid-squat. 'That was actually pretty funny. Usually I do the jokes, thanks. But I'll give you a point for that one.'

Carolyn smirks and sticks her middle finger up at Mel, then picks up her board and launches it over the shore break. The mini mal is a lot heavier than her usual board, so at first it feels awkward and clunky. But the waves are small enough to push the nose of the board over the oncoming whitewater, and she finally gains enough momentum to soar over them quite easily. Perhaps it's a sign of things to come.

Her first visit to Northies hadn't gone nearly as well. It was during the holidays before she started at the Institute of Sporting Excellence. Two older Pacific Grove boys, Chad and Dave, had convinced Carolyn to drive with them to Bonita Shores. She'd thought they were all going there to surf, but when they arrived at the northern car park, they'd told her she should go out and they'd just hang on the beach. At first, she felt uneasy – shark sightings were pretty common here – but then she spotted a few other people in the line-up, so she shrugged and paddled out alone.

The waves were a solid four foot that day, and wobbly due to the mix of swell directions. She knew she'd have to work hard to select the right wave, one nicely formed as opposed to one that would buck you off onto the shallows. She remembers swinging around and taking a late drop, only to hear an onslaught of abuse from behind her over the sound of the breaking waves. Continuing to ride out the left on her forehand, she finished it and turned to see a scruffy-haired boy calling her a 'blow in', pointing his finger to the shore and yelling at her to go in. She hesitated, tempted to paddle back out for one more wave, but saw the rage in his eyes so decided to paddle into the next smaller ride and take it to shore.

Once back on the beach, she could tell by the amount of beer cans surrounding them that Chad and Dave were in no state to drive her home. She grabbed her bag from the back of the car and walked down to the surf club they'd passed on the way in. Unable to find a bus stop, she went inside the reception area. Just as she was being told that there was no bus from Bonita Shores, a girl came out of the bathroom, weaving her long blonde hair into a plait over her shoulder. She asked how the surf was, and Carolyn said it would've been great if she hadn't dropped in on a local by mistake and been ordered in.

The girl asked if the boy had a board with a red bottom and then, when Carolyn nodded, she apologised. That was her brother Tyler, and his bark was way worse than his bite. Carolyn asked if there was a bus to Pacific Grove. The girl shook her head, then told Carolyn she'd be back in a minute. Carolyn was just about to leave when the girl returned with her father, who offered to give Carolyn a lift back out to the Pacific Highway so she could catch a bus. Carolyn wanted to refuse the offer, then realised hitching was her only other option. She couldn't believe two complete strangers were being this kind to her.

On the way to the car, Carolyn saw the blonde girl wave to another girl who was under the club where all the surfboards were stored. This was Carolyn's first interaction with Jaspa and Mel. The next time she saw them was when she started at her new school, two months later.

A bit of water bumps against the rocks and moves towards Carolyn. She lays on the mini mal and takes two strokes into the wave, popping to her feet once she feels the tail of her board begin to lift. She rides down the line, getting in sync with the slowness of the weak swell. She can hear Jaspa and Mel hooting her on as she weaves back and forth along the face of the wave.

Carolyn reaches the back of the line-up to join Jaspa and Mel. 'That turned out to be a sick-as wave,' she says, trying to process all of the good things that were happening to her. She sits upright, straddling her board, which feels like an overweight horse. She's used to a surfboard sinking below the surface, but this one remains afloat above the water. If there was ever a moment when she could understand what being on top of the world feels like, this would be it.

#10

'Dude, I still can't believe we're on the other side of the world.' Carolyn presses her nose against the window of the minivan as it exits Rio de Janeiro airport. Cars honk their horns and zip in and out with far less order than they would in Australia. Even their own driver seems to have little concern for the safety of this van full of school kids.

'Sir, can I ask that you slow down a little please?' Ellen Ryder asks politely.

'Oh, I'm sorry ma'am,' he says, turning to face her and leaving the car's navigation to luck. 'For me, this is slow. But don't you worry,' he adds, turning back to face the front, much to the relief of his passengers, 'I will get you there safely. Never had a crash to this day. And you can call me Rodrigo. Where you from anyway?'

'Australia,' Carolyn, Jaspa and Mel chime together.

'Australia?' he shouts with a high pitch on the last syllable. 'What, with them kangaroos?' He takes his hands off the wheel and forms them into makeshift paws, bobbing up and down in his seat and banging his head against his pine tree-shaped air freshener.

'Oh yeah, we have a kangaroo each,' Mel says, as Carolyn jabs her in the ribs. 'Mine's called Skippy, naturally. Jaspa's is Paw Paw and Carolyn's is Keith.'

'Keith?' Carolyn mouths to Mel, who struggles to contain her giggles.

'What's more, our kangaroos all surf, we taught them as little joeys,' Mel continues, meeting a half amused, half scolding gaze from Jaspa's parents.

'No way, miss, that is incredible, I would surely like to see that.' The driver smiles as wide as his toothy mouth will allow, thrilled by this new information.

'Yeah, and there's even an annual surfing competition where all the kangaroos–'

'Mel,' Anthony says from the back seat. 'Come on, that's enough now. And please, lock your door.'

'Sorry Mr Ryder, I was only playing,' Mel says.

'Why do we need to lock the doors, Dad?' Jaspa asks. 'We never do at home.'

The driver turns around before Anthony has a chance to respond. 'He's right, miss. This country is very beautiful, with lovely people. But some people don't have so much, and they might be stealing your things.'

'It's okay, girls,' Ellen adds as she sees Carolyn clutch onto the money belt that's wrapped around her waist. 'As we talked about earlier, it's just about staying together and staying smart.'

Carolyn thinks back. The last time she stole something was two years ago, a packet of two-minute noodles from the 7-Eleven. Back then, she didn't feel any guilt, and she didn't fear the consequences either. What did she have to lose? It wasn't like she was flogging lipstick. Her theft was for necessary life stuff. Her one rule was that she only stole from large chain stores. It wasn't until she started at the Institute that she felt the gravity of risk involved – suddenly, she could lose something she really cared about. Having a star surfing scholar charged with theft would not be a good look for the school. So, she stopped. It's one of the many things she's hidden from Jaspa and Mel; they don't know their friend used to be a thief. They wouldn't understand, they weren't raised the same way she was.

Carolyn glances out of the window and wonders what it would be like to be a teenager living in Brazil. How many days a week do they go to school? Do they have television? What do they eat on Christmas Day? What kind of pets do they have?

As Rodrigo does what would definitely be an illegal manoeuvre in Australia and overtakes a car while rounding a bend, Carolyn gasps. 'Oh no way, guys, there's the beach!'

'Yes, miss,' Rodrigo says with a grin. 'This is the very famous Copacabana.'

Carolyn sits forward and looks out the front window to see a long stretch of highway with sand on one side and a small city on the other. Beyond the buildings lie a scattering of mountainous peaks. It reminds Carolyn of a compacted version of the Gold Coast. Anthony starts singing a song about Copacabana and a woman named Lola, much to Rodrigo's amusement.

'Hey, Rodrigo, what's it like living in Brazil?' Carolyn asks over Anthony's out-of-key enthusiasm.

'Yes, miss, Brazil is very fun. I was born here in Rio, I have lived here for forty years. I am a *carioca*.'

'Karaoke?' Mel laughs.

'*Carioca* is someone who be from Rio. It is very nice here, we have beach, we have good food, we have party-party.'

'You're forty and you still party?' Mel asks bluntly.

'Yes, miss. Brazilians love party-party. Age is nothing here.'

'What's your house like, Rodrigo?' Carolyn asks.

'It's an apartment, miss, we have two bedrooms. I have my wife and my four children.'

'What, all in a two-bedroom apartment?' Carolyn interrupts.

'Yes, miss.'

Carolyn imagines what it would be like to have to share a bedroom with three siblings. Hectic. 'Do you live close by here?'

'No, miss. I cannot be affording here. I drop you at your hotel and then two hours to my home.'

'Two hours?' Carolyn says, louder than she intended. 'That's so long!'

'Yes, miss. Traffic in Rio can be very bad. Everyone wants to be here. Beach, restaurants, possibilities.'

'Possibilities?' Carolyn asks after a pause. 'What possibilities?'

'Possibility of a better life, miss. But most times they be looking in the wrong places. First they be needing to work out what better means.'

Rodrigo looks in the rear-view mirror and holds Carolyn's gaze. She wonders if he's trying to communicate some deeper meaning. Does he mean there's a better location than this city?

The van weaves through the backstreets. Each block is compacted with a mix of residential homes, hotels and shops, and the sidewalks are busy with people jogging or carrying shopping bags. Carolyn's attention is drawn to a girl skateboarding across the road. *What makes this country so different to Australia?* she wonders.

#11

Carolyn is jolted from her thoughts as Rodrigo recklessly crosses oncoming traffic to pull into a hotel driveway.

'Is this it, are we here?' Mel asks excitedly as they arrive at Hotel Carnival de Rio. Two men wearing dark blue suits with gold buttons and little round hats rush to the van and unload their luggage onto a trolley. Outside, the building looks old, with arched windows and vines creeping up cracked walls. But inside, the foyer is like something out of a luxury travel brochure. Large white pots housing tropical plants that are taller than Carolyn rest on the grey speckled marble flooring. It feels a bit affluent for somewhere a bunch of surfers will be staying.

A tall woman wearing bright red lipstick greets them from behind the reception desk.

'*Olá, como vai você?*' she asks. 'Welcome to Rio.'

Carolyn stands back, listening to Anthony attempt his Aussie bogan Portuguese to check them in. She snorts to herself, thinking how Jaspa's so lucky, not only to have a dad, but to have one who's so cool and playful.

'Hey, you guys beat us,' Carolyn hears from behind her. She turns to see Thomas Sampson and the rest of the junior surf team entering the foyer.

'Yeah,' Carolyn says. 'Our driver would've got like twenty speeding tickets if we were back home.'

'It's fully like Asia 'n that,' says Wil Sanders, the team's best aerial surfer.

'Yeah,' Carolyn agrees, and leaves it at that. She's never been to Asia, and she's not in the mood for the *oh you gotta go, it's so sick* response to her truth. It's much easier to cut conversations short.

She walks over to where Jaspa and Mel sit on the foyer couch. 'Dude, I just hit a wall, I'm so freakin' tired,' she says as they shuffle over so she can flop down beside them.

'Me too.' Jaspa trails the last word off into a big yawn, cupping her mouth with her hand as she exhales.

'Don't do that,' Mel protests, her words also disappearing into a yawn. 'It's totes contagious.'

They laugh and look away from each other's yawns, as Anthony and Ellen approach them.

'You girls look as beat as we feel,' Anthony says, placing an arm around Ellen. 'Let's go upstairs and settle in, and we'll meet the rest of the team for an early dinner.'

Carolyn feels her mouth water. Now she can't think about anything *but* food. 'I wonder what we'll eat,' she says to Jaspa and Mel as they follow the bellboy to the lifts.

Mel smirks. 'Ah, that's our girl. I was wondering how long it would take you to bring up food.'

'Well the airplane meal was crap. And that must've been about seven hours ago by now. I want a schnitty.'

'I want a shower,' Jaspa says, pinching her loose top and shaking it to allow airflow. 'It's so much hotter here than home.'

'Hello,' Carolyn replies, pointing down at her long-sleeved top and jeans, then widening her eyes in search of sympathy.

'But you wear that in forty-degree east coast heat,' Mel says, giving her a playful shove.

They get into the lift with Jaspa's parents, and the

bellboy stops outside with their trolley of luggage. 'No room, I get the next one,' he says politely.

Ellen holds the lift open with her hand. 'No, no, come in, please, there's plenty of room.'

'Yeah, we'll all squeeze in, it's fine,' Mel says. 'It'll just be like surfing Snapper Rocks.'

The three girls giggle as they mimic paddling so their arms are touching each other, saying 'oi' and calling out for imaginary waves.

The lift reaches the fifth floor and pings as the doors slide open. The bellboy struggles up the corridor, wrestling with their surfboards and luggage but refusing their offers of help. The interior upstairs looks older than the foyer. The carpet is brown with an orange hexagon pattern, and Carolyn detects the same musty smell that's present in her home after it's been raining. The walls are a pale mint green and covered in pictures of Copacabana beach from the 1950s, featuring Brazilian women wearing much bigger bikinis than they do now.

Carolyn follows everyone into room 54 and takes it all in. Ellen and Anthony have their luggage placed in the double room, while the three girls have their own adjoining area that hosts three single beds. Carolyn is thrilled to see there's a balcony. Opening the sliding door and stepping outside, she's met by the sound of traffic and people laughing. She can see a glimpse of the ocean through the gaps between other buildings. A balcony is the one thing Carolyn believes would make her own home bearable. She wouldn't even care what view it offered, as long as it meant she could go outside and get a different perspective.

'Ready, girls?' Anthony asks as Jaspa exits the bathroom, towel-drying her wet hair.

Carolyn considers changing, but she doesn't want to delay the dinner proceedings any further. 'Yep, I'm ready,' she replies, picking up her wallet and trying to shove it into the back pocket of her jeans.

'Leave that here, love,' Ellen says, waving her hand at Carolyn. 'We'll get dinner.'

Carolyn whispers a surprised thank you and they all take the lift down to the hotel's restaurant, Horizonte Azul.

'I guess that means blue horizon,' Mel says.

'Why do they speak Portuguese in Brazil, but Spanish in other South American countries?' Carolyn asks Anthony as they walk over to the rest of the Australian surf team.

'Because the first European settlers in Brazil were from Portugal, whereas the rest of South American was settled by Spaniards.'

'Ah, righto,' Carolyn nods. 'Wow, what's the dealio

here?' she says, eyeing off a long table packed with numerous dishes of food.

A man not much taller than Carolyn finishes talking to Thomas Sampson then swings around to face them. He's wearing a Rip Curl T-shirt and has tattoos covering both arms, including a fish, flowers, a woman's face, a dragon and more flowers.

'Hello,' the man says with a strong accent, holding out his hand for Anthony to shake. 'I am Carlos, I am the contest coordinator. Anything you need you just say, "Yo, Carlos," okay?'

'Sounds good, great to meet you,' Anthony says, shaking Carlos's hand.

'So, in Brazil we do buffets, you know them?' Carlos says.

Carolyn nods, her sudden hunger almost rendering her speechless. 'Yeah, there's a buffet at the Grove's RSL.'

'Here you just get a plate, there is the meat, there is the fish, there is the salad,' Carlos explains, pointing around the room. 'You pile your plate and then it is weighed and you pay per pound.'

'Oh,' Carolyn says, realising she'll have to show some restraint so Mrs Ryder doesn't get a nasty shock when the bill comes. She does a lap of the tables, viewing each dish and working out her priorities. The braised beef is number one in her mind, that is until she sees the sticky barbecued chicken wings. Perhaps just one of each, she convinces herself. Jaspa glides past, her plate piled high with salad. Carolyn reaches for the shredded slaw and covers her meat so it can't be seen. She understands Jaspa's reasons for becoming a vegetarian, but she can't get there herself. If there's a spread of meat before her, juicy and succulent, especially one that she doesn't have to pay for, she's going in.

'What's that?' Carolyn asks, pointing to Mel's plate as she sits down opposite her and Jaspa.

'I actually have no idea,' Mel says, spearing the small golden ball onto her fork and offering it to Carolyn. 'Here, try it. You know you want to.'

Carolyn pinches it off the fork and inspects it, then takes a bite and struggles with the chewiness. 'Oh, dude, it's kinda weird,' she says, inspecting the ball. 'It's like bread.'

'It is bread,' says a voice from behind her. 'It's *pão de queijo*, our Brazilian cheese bread.' The girl is sitting at the table behind them with five guys.

'Oh, thanks, yeah, cheese,' Carolyn says with a single nod of her head, turning back to pick up a chicken wing, keen to avoid a conversation with people she doesn't know.

'Who's that?' Mel asks while attempting to chew through the cheese bread.

'I dunno.' Carolyn shrugs, and continues to eat.

'Come on, there are five hotties sitting at that table, you could've been our in. Lift your game, chick.'

Carolyn shrugs. She knows Mel's joking, but she can also feel the expectation in her comment. Carolyn so often feels she can't measure up to Mel's standards. Her most hideous moments are the times she's expected to contribute to a conversation but says something dumb or weird, or cuts herself off mid-sentence for fear she's not making sense. Or worse still, when someone asks her something deeply personal about herself and then sits back and waits for a response as though they've just asked her the way to the shops. Stuff that. You let people in, they'll tear up your insides. Carolyn's insides are already fragile enough.

12

'Jesus,' Mel says.

'Whoa,' Jaspa agrees.

'Dude,' Carolyn whispers, secretly wishing she'd slept in.

The three girls stand at the shore, leaning against their upright surfboards.

'There must be a hundred suckers out there,' Mel says.

'Maybe even more.' Carolyn cringes as they watch five surfers paddle onto the one wave and all take off at the same time. Two fall mid-air and don't make the drop, two collide at the base of the wave in a race to get around the whitewater, while the remaining surfer flies down the line and carves a big hack into the end section.

'Hey, that's the chick from the Brazilian table last night,' Mel says. 'She rips.'

'Yeah, she shreds.' Carolyn uses her foot to shovel a hole in the sand. 'So, are we really doing this? It's totally closing out.'

Jaspa jiggles on the spot. 'Come on, it'll be fun. The water's gorgeous and Dad, Tyler and Cooper are already out there.'

Carolyn attaches her leg-rope to her ankle then mumbles, 'Okay, we're doing it then.' She wades in up to her waist, pushing her board over the whitewater. The water's warm, and she enjoys the silkiness of it against her belly, exposed between her bikini top and boardshorts.

The line-up is chaotic, but she waits for a gap between sets then paddles furiously out the back to avoid being run over.

'You made it,' Anthony laughs as she strokes over to where the Australian team huddles, then sits upright on her board.

'It's hectic out here,' she says, taking it all in. She's surfed in crowds this big before, the few times she's gone to the Gold Coast point breaks. But there, everyone is spread out. Here, everyone's scrambling on the one bank with a mix of pro junior surfers from the tour and complete beginners. 'We just saw five people dropping in on each other.'

'Okay, girls,' Anthony says, waving Mel and Jaspa over to join them. 'Stay close and we can all take turns.'

'Sure, it's crowded,' Mel says as they straddle their boards and use their hands to wade closer to each other. 'But can you actually believe we're surfing in Rio de Janeiro?' The shoreline is packed with high-rise apartments, and various green mountain peaks serve as the city's backdrop. 'It's pretty freakin' beautiful.'

Carolyn thinks back to just a few weeks ago, when she thought she would have to leave professional surfing before it even really began. Now she's on the other side of the world, in a country where they speak another language, have different money, and she's trying food she's never eaten before. Carolyn digs deep to find the excitement, but every time she relaxes into the idea that she deserves to be here, she thinks back to the mystery cheque. What if someone chases her down and demands the money back? Sometimes it's easier not to have things, so there's no risk of them being whipped away from you.

She hears a whistle from behind her. 'Carolyn, this one's yours,' Mel screams over the sound of several people speaking Portuguese.

A bump in the ocean moves towards her. Several other surfers scramble to get into position but they're too far out the back. Tyler growls at the other surfers to back off, so Carolyn grabs the nose of her board and uses her feet to propel herself from the water and glide tummy-first onto her surfboard. Two strokes of her hands and she gains speed with the pitching lip, whipping her head from left to right to assess which direction to take. A guy on the right-hander paddles his softboard wide-legged and bounces into the wave on his belly, so Carolyn guides herself in the opposite direction and pops to her feet to travel left. She takes a high line across the face, using weight in her front foot to generate speed. It reminds her of all the times she's played 'beat the closeout' with Mel and Jaspa at Pacific Grove's most open beach, where they take on the notoriously dumpy waves to practise their quick take-offs and try to find the green section before the whitewash swallows them up.

A shut-down section approaches, so she straightens her board towards shore and remains standing until she reaches the shallows. There are too many human obstacles to avoid if she paddles back out, so she decides to sit on the beach and wait for the others to come in. Leaving her leg-rope attached and her knees bent, she flops back onto the sand, close enough so the ocean laps over her toes, and allows her eyelids to fold shut.

A drop of water lands on Carolyn's face. And then another. She squints up into the sun to see a figure standing over her and jolts upright.

'Hey,' says a voice.

Carolyn's eyes regain focus and she realises it's the cheese bread girl from last night. Before she can make up an excuse to leave, the girl sits down next to her.

'Did you get waves?' the girl asks in English.

'Yeah, but nah,' Carolyn replies, staring straight ahead.

'Sorry, I don't understand. Is this yes or no you catching the waves?'

Carolyn keeps her head still but shifts her gaze to the girl. Is she really expecting a reply? The crinkle in the girl's small, triangular nose and squinted smile suggests she's hoping the conversation will continue.

'Oh, sorry, yeah. One. But it was a closeout.' Carolyn wonders if the girl will understand Australian surfing terminology. A look of recognition and agreement forms across the girl's face. Maybe it is a universal language?

'Yes, this is crap spot,' the girl says matter-of-factly.

Carolyn huffs out a laugh at the accent lining the profanity.

'There are many other good beaches for surfing. Are you in competition?'

Carolyn nods. 'Yep, you?'

'*Sim*, yes. I am on Brazilian team. Are you English?'

'Australian.'

'Oh, I always want to go there. So many waves. I hear, so many good waves. Where we go for the contest tomorrow, Praia do Rosa, it is very good wave, and very beautiful place.'

Carolyn didn't realise they were going somewhere else for the competition. She'd thought this was it, and had been finding it difficult to get excited. She already feels insecure about having her surfing on display, let alone trying to generate a score from a shut-down wave in front of the world's best junior surfers.

'I must go. He is my coach,' says the girl, raising her hand to a man who's walking up the beach with two other surfers, carrying a tripod. 'What is your name?'

'Carolyn.'

'Mine is Thais. Like Thai and add s.'

Carolyn's shoulders stiffen as the girl leans in and brushes her lips against one cheek and then the other.

'Goodbye, Carolyn.'

Carolyn watches Thais walk away, weirded out at being kissed goodbye by someone she only just met. She waits on the beach as Mel, Jaspa, Anthony, Tyler and Cooper all catch a party wave together and ride to shore.

As they make their way back to the hotel, the streets bustle with women dressed as though they're going out clubbing, even though it's only 9 am. Carolyn feels out of place carrying a surfboard while wearing boardshorts and a bikini, and she's relieved when they finally reach the hotel foyer and take the lift up to their room.

'Hi, Mum,' Jaspa says as they walk through the door to see Ellen sitting in a chair on the balcony reading a book.

'Hi, team,' she replies, removing her red square-framed reading glasses. 'How was the surf?'

'Straight-handers,' Carolyn replies as Mel pushes past her and Jaspa to beat them to the shower.

Anthony leans down to give Ellen a kiss on the forehead. 'Have you eaten, love?'

Ellen shakes her head and offers a warm smile. 'No, not yet. But Thomas stopped by to let us know that the team are on their way back from the beach and we're to meet in the auditorium at 9:30 for breakfast and a briefing on tomorrow.'

'Righto, you lot,' Anthony calls from the balcony. 'Three-minute showers, max, and ready to roll in fifteen.'

Carolyn tries to not drip too much on the carpet as she walks into the bedroom to see Mel slipping into a denim skirt and aqua tank top. 'Who's in there now?' Carolyn asks, pointing to the bathroom.

'Jaspa's using the other shower and Cooper's in there.'

Carolyn bangs on the bathroom door. 'Carn, dude, time's up.'

The door opens. 'Sorry,' Cooper says, tip-toeing over the floor while clutching the towel that's wrapped around his waist.

Carolyn steps into the bathroom and undresses, then looks around and groans. 'Seriously?' Her towel is in a soggy pile on the floor, having been inconsiderately used as a bath mat. 'Damn it.' She cracks open the door.

'Mel!'

Waits.

'Mel!'

Waits, then yells, 'Mel!'

'Jesus, what?' Mel says, walking back in from the balcony.

'Pass me that towel, mine's soaked.'

'Why didn't you just walk over and get it yourself?'

'Cos I've got no clothes on.'

'So, who cares?'

'I care. Just pass me the freakin' towel would ya?'

Mel picks up her towel from the bed, holds it

against her cheek then chucks it to Carolyn. 'It's a bit damp.'

Carolyn catches it gratefully. 'Better than soaked. Thanks.' Great, her three-minute shower has now diminished to one. She turns on the tap and blasts her front, then quickly her back, towels herself dry and changes into a clean pair of boardshorts and a grey rayon T-shirt.

Once she's slipped into her thongs they all make their way down to the ground level. 'That Brazilian chick from last night said our next stop has sick waves,' Carolyn says to Mel and Jaspa as they find a table and sit together.

The room is full of people who all obviously have one thing in common: they're all pro junior surfers.

'Dad says where we're going has a lot less people too, and is kind of like between Bonita Shores and Byron Bay,' Jaspa says, scooping a spoonful of eggs and beans onto her plate.

'Wahoo, if it's like Byron! Hope you packed your party shoes, girls,' Mel says, dancing her hands above her head. 'Oh, shh, shh,' she adds, holding a finger up to her lip. 'They're about to start.'

Carolyn scoffs a quiet laugh to herself, amused that Mel's doing the shushing when she was the one talking.

'Welcome to Brazil,' says Carlos, tapping his chest with his fists and holding them in the air. 'I'm so happy to have you in my country. Tomorrow we will fly to Floripa, then shuttle buses will take us south to Praia do Rosa – or if you want to be like local, we sometimes call Rosa, pronounced with a *ho*. The surfing will be very good, you will like this place, it is very beautiful. Your drivers will take you straight to La Playa Resort, we all stay there. The competition starts the next day.'

Mel playfully kicks Carolyn and Jaspa under the table and they exchange a look of wide-eyed excitement.

Noise starts to trickle around the room as surfers anticipate their impending adventures. Carlos claps his hands several times to regain everyone's attention. 'Okay, okay.' His voice booms, bringing the room to silence. 'This is important, please keep attention. Brazil will give you a good time, and Rosa is a safe place, but you must always stay in groups and watch out for each other. *Entende?* You understand? Okay, continue your breakfast, and enjoy Brazil's delicious *pão de queijo*,' he says, picking one up from the closest table and popping it in his mouth. 'You will never get tired of these.'

'I'm not convinced about those cheese balls yet,' Carolyn says as Mel flicks one onto Carolyn's plate.

'But you'll eat it anyway, right?' Mel asks, as she bites into one and stretches out the dough.

'Heck yeah,' Carolyn says, dipping hers into the beans on her plate. As she swirls the cheese bread around and leans forward to scoop it up into her mouth, someone catches her eye. There's a man sitting with the Brazilian surf team on the other side of the room, and he seems to be staring straight at her.

#13

Carolyn shuffles in her seat and lowers her gaze.

'What's up?' Mel says, swivelling in her chair to look behind her, and then back at Carolyn.

'Huh? Oh, nothing.' Carolyn's eyes dart across the crowd. The man is now looking down at his phone. Perhaps she just imagined it. 'Ya know, just scoping the room.'

'For food or dudes?' Mel laughs.

Jaspa reaches over the table to squeeze Carolyn's wrist. 'You sure you're okay? You look a bit spooked.'

'Yeah, nah, I'm sweet.' Carolyn swiftly brushes off the attention. 'Can I go for food *and* dudes?' she replies to Mel in order to shift the focus away from Jaspa, who may pick up she's out of sorts.

Mel retrieves her paw paw ointment from her pocket. 'Well, you know my motto,' she says, squeezing balm onto her finger to rub across her lips. 'We can have it all.' She smacks her lips together, chucks the tube to Carolyn, then gets up to go to the toilet.

Carolyn picks up the tube, pinches it between her thumb and forefinger and plays with it rather than applying it. She taps the base on the table and slides her hand from top to bottom, then flips it over to do it again. Mel's words ring through her ears. *We can have it all.* Carolyn wonders what her *all* would be. A bigger home? A bigger bank account? A more functional family? But Carolyn rarely allows herself to think big. If you don't want for it then there's no risk of disappointment when it doesn't happen. She's endured years of any slight glimpse of desire being batted back down by her mum. 'People like us don't get this', 'People like us don't get that'. But why should the four walls you live in reflect who you are as a person?

'Can I please have some of that once you're done?' Jaspa asks Carolyn.

'Huh?'

'The paw paw,' Jaspa says. 'Can I have some please?'

'Oh, sure.' She spins it across the table to Jaspa.

'So,' Mel interrupts, sliding back into her seat. 'I

just spoke to Thommo, and we're going for a little sight-seeing adventure with the rest of the team.'

Ellen and Anthony approach the table. 'Are you girls ready?' Anthony says. 'We're going to all take a little road trip and make the most of this gorgeous day. Run upstairs and grab your wallets. Remember, only take the money you need today.'

Carolyn, Mel and Jaspa bolt to the lift, shouting at Tyler and Cooper to hold the door for them. In a flash, they've collected their money and are piling into their minivan. They drive back onto the highway. What a relief, the onshore wind is ripping across the beach. It's so much easier to enjoy out-of-ocean activities when the surf is crappy. No surf FOMO today.

A bubble of emotion bobs around in Carolyn's belly. She can't work out if it's anxiety or excitement about being in a different country. As they wind through the streets, she peers out through the van window and tries to conjure up a make-believe profile of everyone they pass. The three old men playing checkers on the side of the road. The girl who looks close to Carolyn's age, waiting at the bus stop holding a baby on her hip. The skinny young man walking from car to car, trying to convince drivers to let him wipe their windscreen in return for cash.

They come to a stop at the lights and are swarmed by a group of young boys holding their cupped hands up to the window.

'Don't open the windows, girls,' Thomas warns from the front seat.

'Why, what do they want?' Carolyn asks, looking straight into the dark, saucer-shaped eyes of one boy who seems to be mouthing 'please'.

'They want money, but we've been told not to give them any. It encourages them to be on the streets instead of at school.'

Carolyn is torn. Would they really be begging like this if they didn't need help? They're just little kids. She mouths 'sorry' to the boy. He comes closer to the van, his eyes a puddle of water, and holds his hands higher so they touch the window. Carolyn places her palm against the glass and mouths 'sorry' again as the van starts to move forward. The boy jerks his hands away with a vitriolic glare.

'Whoa, did you see that?' Mel leans forward from the seat behind Carolyn. 'He was not happy with you.'

'Poor little dude, I wish I could've given him something.'

'I know, but Thommo said we shouldn't encourage them.'

'Yo, but how desperate do you have to be to go up to cars in the middle of the street and beg? Not helping them is a dumbass rule.'

Thomas swivels from the front seat and takes a deep breath, which he always does when he's about to say something profound. 'It's complicated, girls. It's heartbreaking not to be able to give to those in need, especially in a country like Brazil that struggles with the extremes of those who are incredibly rich and those who are devastatingly poor.'

The girls fall silent for a moment, and Carolyn feels the weight of guilt press against her chest. 'But what does it freakin' matter if we just gave them two bucks each? That could be their dinner.' There she'd been, all worried about not being able to go on tour, and at the click of her fingers not only her friends but also the town of Bonita Shores had come to her rescue.

Ellen leans across the aisle of the van and squeezes Carolyn's wrist. 'As Thomas said, sweetheart, it's really complicated. What you don't want is to create an industry where the parents of these children think it's more financially beneficial for them to be begging on the streets than to be in school.'

Carolyn glances at Mel and Jaspa. They're all privileged, not only to go to school, but to go to a school where they get to surf. Carolyn hoists her knee up on the seat to face Ellen and chews on a fingernail. 'But how is school going to put dinner on their plate?'

'Well, put it this way,' Ellen says. 'What do you think is one of the main things that can prevent poverty?'

'Money trees,' Jaspa says. 'Or all the rich people have to pay a poverty tax.'

Mel scoffs. 'That ain't ever going to happen.'

'Mel's right, sadly. A share in wealth is unlikely from the greedy. But education can be incredibly empowering. For knowledge, collaboration, a sense of achievement, being exposed to possibilities. It's a long-term investment though, and one that also needs the support of our political leaders.'

Carolyn's mind is racing. Until she started at the Institute she always thought of school and her part-time job as chores, just items on life's to-do list, rather than something of privilege. She's still deep in thought when the van winds its way up a mountain and pulls to a stop in a car park.

'This is it, we're here,' Thomas announces, brushing a flop of hair away from his eyes.

'Where are we? We're so high up in the hills!' Jaspa says as they file one-by-one out of the van.

'You'll find out soon enough.' Thomas smiles.

'*Olá,*' Carolyn hears from behind her. She swings around to see Thais standing next to her, adjusting the denim shorts that cut almost above her bum cheeks. She's shorter than Carolyn, but her stance is powerful. Muscular legs that seem to almost grip the ground, like they would never fumble out of place, and shoulders that look pinned back in comparison to Carolyn's slumped posture.

'Yo, hey,' Carolyn says, fidgeting with the wallet in her pocket. Damn, she should've put it in her travel pouch, now she's going to be paranoid all day about losing it. 'How's it goin'?'

'I like your hat, it suits you,' Thais says with an endearing bluntness.

'Oh,' Carolyn says, grabbing the peak of her grey and blue trucker hat to turn it around. 'Thanks.' What's the etiquette here, should she respond with a compliment, is that a Brazilian thing to do? Rather than stumble and blurt out something weird, Carolyn changes the subject. 'So, what are you guys doing here?'

'We are all here, all the surf teams are here for the group photo.'

'Photo?'

'*Sim,* photo. Do you know where we are?'

Carolyn shrugs. 'Nup, where are we?'

'Okay, come, you see soon, we walk with everybody.'

A big cluster of fit, tanned teenagers and their adult chaperones walk up a steep hill, announcing themselves with excited conversation and playful wrestling. As they round a bend Carolyn looks up and gasps.

'Jesus!' she blurts, not realising her choice of words is perfect.

'Yes, this is Cristo,' Thais says, placing an arm around Carolyn's shoulders. 'A sight you will never forget.'

Carolyn rotates to take in the view. The towering white statue of Christ the Redeemer, arms flung wide, stands tall above them at the highest point of the mountain. Carolyn and Thais are shuffled into the front row of the photo, posed with the other ninety-three surfers. Carolyn looks over and laughs at Mel, who is holding two middle fingers up to the camera. Carolyn can't wait to see the photograph, all of them standing in front of this massive statue with a blue-sky backdrop.

'Come,' Thais says, taking Carolyn by the arm. 'I show you special spot.'

Carolyn stiffens. 'Oh, I'd rather wait for Mel and Jaspa.'

'Well, we ask them,' Thais says warmly, still holding

onto Carolyn's arm. 'Come, come.' She waves them over with her other hand.

Mel and Jaspa join them, and Carolyn shuffles awkwardly as Thais leans in to give them each a kiss on the cheek. She kicks at the dirt, wondering how someone can be so forthright with people she's just met. Mel and Jaspa don't seem to mind, though. They walk on ahead, trudging further up the hill, arms linked with Thais.

Jaspa looks back at Carolyn. 'Come on, slow coach!'

Carolyn follows them under a railing and down an embankment. They're soon in a secluded spot, out of view of the tourists bustling above.

'Dude,' Carolyn says as she joins the three girls to sit on a rock. She's never seen a view this incredible before. Not even at the top of Mount Warning, where it's Australian bush as far as the eye can see. This is a spectacular meeting of hills, winding shorelines, dense buildings and tall green islands scattered across the ocean. Carolyn is struck by the contradiction in the beauty; all those people living in such close proximity, fighting for their bit of paradise.

'See down there,' Thais says, pointing to the right. 'That's where we surfed this morning.'

'Or at least tried to,' Mel laughs.

'It's so much prettier than I pictured,' Jaspa says, holding up her phone to take a panoramic shot.

'What are all those houses up there on the hill?' Carolyn asks. 'They'd have a mad view.'

'Have you heard of favela?' Thais asks. The girls shake their heads. 'It means slum. This is for very poor people. If they don't have money for a home, they make a life there in the favela. It is like a mini city, but very basic – sometimes no water, sometimes houses made from scrap. It can be dangerous, with bad people and drug problems.'

Carolyn stares up at the favela, deep in thought, wondering if it's like her block of housing commission flats at home. 'Does the government help pay, like a concession?'

Thais furrows her brow and a look of disgust crosses her face. 'Our government is crap. It is corrupt. It will do nothing to help these people. It helps rich people and the politicians' own needs. This is big problem in Brazil. There are hundreds and hundreds of these favelas all over Rio.'

'Hundreds?' Mel asks, loud enough to startle the passers-by above them. 'Jesus.'

Carolyn fidgets in silence, staring at the tiny, unevenly built homes, stacked tightly up the face of the mountain. She wonders if this is where those boys who were begging at the lights are from. 'Have you always lived in Copacabana?' Carolyn asks Thais.

'No,' Thais says, hanging her head and allowing her dark, wavy hair to fall over her face. 'I was born there,' she says, pointing at the hill. 'In the favela.'

#14

Carolyn is sprawled across the back seat of the van, drifting between sleep and a jetlagged haze. As they pull into the hotel car park, she senses a presence, prompting her to open her eyes.

'What the heck?' she says, wiping drool from her chin with the back of her hand.

Mel and Jaspa are leaning over her, giggling as Mel holds a phone above Carolyn's face.

'I think we definitely got your best angle,' Mel says, using her fingers to pinch the screen and edit the picture.

'Oh, you bloody did not,' Carolyn says, overcoming her tiredness to bolt upright and reach for Mel's phone.

Mel quickly pulls it back. 'Oh, we bloody did too. Hello, Insta stories.'

Carolyn groans, then slowly gets up and follows the others out of the van. Mel knows she hates her picture being posted online, but the thing about Mel is, she's got a selective memory – especially when it comes to her own entertainment. The last time Carolyn blew up at her, when Mel posted a video of her tripping over her leg-rope and face-planting into the sand, should have been enough to deter her, but apparently not. Carolyn has no desire to be in the spotlight or anywhere near it. The more people who can see you, the more your imperfections can be judged.

Carolyn walks into the hotel foyer and immediately gets lost in the sea of surfers that crowd the space. She pauses for a moment, looking around for Mel and Jaspa. If there's anywhere Carolyn should feel like part of a tribe, it's here, among this group of professional junior surfers, all hoping to one day qualify for the main tour. But even in this setting, she teeters on the edge of being exposed as a misfit. Soon, someone will discover she's not a great surfer. They'll find out she has to rely on a scholarship to compete, that she doesn't care about make-up or dresses, that she doesn't have a boyfriend. That she doesn't really like people all that much.

Carolyn stifles a yawn. The weight of worrying about being busted as a fraud is exhausting. She spies Mel and Jaspa in front of the lift, listening intently to

Thais, who is talking to them with exaggerated hand gestures. She's noticed that Brazilians seem to do most things with a lot of passion, even just little things like giving directions or a waiter taking a customer's order. It almost makes Carolyn feel emotionally inadequate. She can't conjure up that kind of excitement, even for the things that warrant it.

As Carolyn approaches the others, Thais glances away from the conversation and meets her sleepy gaze. Carolyn feels a wave of warmth roll through her, the kind she only experiences when she sees someone she really cares about. There aren't many people in Carolyn's life who trigger that sensation – Mel, Jaspa and her family, Mr Sampson, her boss. Certainly not somebody she met a day ago. That's just weird.

'Carolyn, you made it to us,' Thais says, placing an arm around her shoulders. That's another thing Carolyn has noticed about Brazilians, they're not big on the concept of personal space. 'We thought you had found somewhere to take sleep,' Thais says.

Although Carolyn reflexively flinches from Thais' touch, it doesn't actually make her feel uncomfortable. Thais is like a mix of Carolyn's two best friends: she has the kindness and compassion of Jaspa, and the intensity and daring of Mel. Before meeting Mel and Jaspa, Carolyn didn't have many female friends. She was always drawn to the boys, familiar with the barriers they build to ward off vulnerability.

'Nah, all good, I was just cruising. Jetlag is a bitch. Do you feel rank as well?'

'Here, try this.' Jaspa rummages through her hessian tote, pulls out a small bottle and unscrews the lid. 'Open your mouth.'

'No way, what the heck is that?' Carolyn says, jerking away from Jaspa.

'Mum got this made up, it's a herbal mix to help with jetlag. Come on, it's fine.' Jaspa holds the dropper over Carolyn's reluctantly open mouth and squeezes three drops of liquid under her tongue.

Carolyn's face contorts in disgust. 'Oh, that's freakin' putrid. It's like the worst medicine I've ever had. Quick, gimme that,' she says, snatching Mel's water bottle and taking a swig.

'I want to try,' Thais says to Jaspa, opening her mouth.

'Are you jetlagged too?' Jaspa says innocently, even though she knows Thais lives in Rio.

'No, but I like to try everything once. Or twice if I really like.' She smiles as Jaspa drops the concoction under her tongue. 'Ooh, it's how you say, very better.'

'Bitter,' Carolyn corrects her. 'It's like all of the foulest bitters in the world bottled up.'

'Well, it works,' Jaspa says, screwing the cap back on. 'I feel fabulous.'

'But you're always bright and shiny,' Mel says, reaching up to pinch Jaspa's cheek. 'That's why we often want to vomit on you.'

'You three are cute,' Thais says. 'You seem like best friends.'

'Cos we are,' the three girls chorus.

'I want to show you something special, can you come?' Thais asks them, raising her eyebrows.

'I'm so sorry, I've been neglecting Cooper so I promised I'd meet him' for a game of Bananagrams before dinner,' Jaspa tells an incredibly confused-looking Thais. 'It's a word game,' Jaspa clarifies. 'Like Scrabble. Mum and Dad got us into it and we're a bit addicted.' Jaspa bends down to draw them all into a hug. 'But I'll see you for dinner.'

Mel looks at her phone and smiles. 'Although I hate to break the code and ditch my chicks, that hottie over there has been dropping into my DMs, so I'm obliged to at least give him a chance to meet the girl of his dreams.' Mel nods towards a group of guys sitting in the lounge area, all engrossed in their phones.

'Which one?' Thais asks.

Mel points. 'The one in red.'

'Okay, he is good guy, on my surf team. Many

Brazilian guys are cheating, but he is not them.'

'Roger that.'

'No, his name is not Roger it is Luis.'

Mel and Carolyn laugh.

'Roger is just something we say when we understand something. Like, I say I'm off to hook up with a hottie and you reply, okay, roger that. Oh, and here he comes. I'll see you chicks later.' Mel disappears.

Thais turns to Carolyn. 'So, just us then?'

Carolyn shrugs. 'I guess. What are we doing exactly?'

'Come, I show you.' Thais presses the button for the lift.

Carolyn hesitates, then says, 'I'm kinda not supposed to stray without the team. Are we staying in the hotel?'

'You'll see.' The lift door pings open and Thais grabs Carolyn's hand and leads her in. 'I promise we won't be long, and it will be worth it.'

Thais presses the button for the top floor and the doors close, leaving them alone in the lift. Carolyn leans back against the handrail and peers at Thais from beneath the peak of her trucker cap.

'Do you live with your mum and dad?' Carolyn asks, surprised at herself. She usually avoids any interest in other people's personal information.

'I live with my *papai*, my father. My mother took off back to Japan when I was only *cinco*,' Thais says, holding up five fingers.

'Oh, that sucks. So, your mum's Japanese?' Carolyn says, realising why Thais looks so exotic.

'*Sim*, my *mãe* is from Shikoku island, and *Papai* is a carioca, which means–'

'He's from Rio,' Carolyn cuts in, feeling somewhat worldly.

'Yes, how you know this?' Thais asks, visibly impressed.

'Our taxi driver told us when we first rocked up here. So, do you see your mum much?' The lift pings on the tenth floor, leaving her question lingering in the air as they step out to the open patio, where they're greeted by the joyful sound of hotel guests enjoying the pool area, dive bombing into the water and shouting over the top of one another.

'Come,' Thais says, taking Carolyn's wrist and leading her away from the pool area and around the side of the hotel. Thais stops short at a narrow entrance where two buildings meet and whispers to Carolyn, 'I hope you don't have that thing, that fear of small places?'

'Claustrophobia?' Carolyn says. 'No. I mean, I don't love them but, no.'

Carolyn puts her wallet in her pocket and turns on her side to follow Thais through the crack, shuffling against the coolness of the wall. They're almost at the end when Thais stops.

'We go through here.'

Carolyn looks up at the small square hole cut into the wall. 'Dude, how?'

'It's okay, it looks high, but the ground is close over there. Watch.' Thais wrenches herself up onto the hole and uses her hands to scuffle headfirst through to the other side. 'See, *simples*.' After a pause. 'You coming?'

Carolyn bites her bottom lip. All her instincts are telling her to abort the mission and head back to the others. Why should she trust someone she barely knows? But she really wants to go. She doesn't know why exactly, but she knows she wants to.

'Yo, coming,' Carolyn calls, shoving her wallet further into her pocket. She hoists herself up onto the wall and crawls through to the other side, where Thais helps her onto the ground.

'See? Easy!' Thais says. 'The way back is trickier because the ground is lower on that side, but we help each other.'

And to Carolyn's utter surprise, she finds that she not only believes Thais, she trusts her.

'Before, you asked me about my mother,' Thais says as they jump onto a narrow brick wall and tightrope walk to the end. 'Where I am taking you will explain many things. Come, we go through here.'

A long undercover walkway stretches ahead of them, extending beyond their line of sight. Thais bends down and removes a loosened square of the plastic that covers the tunnel. It reminds Carolyn of the tunnel at Sea World, that runs between the two pools so visitors can see fish and sharks swimming all around them. But this is in the middle of the city. What the heck is it?

They ease themselves through the hole to step onto the floor.

'It closes at five,' Thais says, 'so the tourists will be gone by now.'

'What is it?' Carolyn asks as they walk along the tunnel. There's a clear view below them of a lush hotel garden with towering palm trees surrounding a human-made lagoon, complete with a rocky border, trickling waterfall and quaint bridge. Waiters serve men dressed in linen and women wearing designer bikinis and far too much jewellery for poolside activities.

'This the Resort de Ouro, the most expensive hotel in Rio. But come.'

Carolyn quickens her pace to keep up with Thais as they follow the walkway for another five minutes. Carolyn's watch blinks 5:05 pm. She'll need to be back by six at the latest to avoid getting busted. She checks her phone. No one has tried to contact her, so she's in the clear so far.

Their surroundings begin to change rapidly as they ascend a hill. The leafy suburb and immaculately main-tained apartments below them are replaced by a mass of small, brown-brick homes, all stacked on top of each other, stretching to the top of the hill. As they draw closer, Carolyn can see the buildings are a patchwork of material. Sheets of corrugated iron serve as roofs, many of them punctured with rusting holes, and washing is messily hung out to dry on drooping ropes. Small chil-dren in ripped dirty clothes run around the narrow streets as busy adults carry buckets of water, cook in the street on portable stoves and sit in deck chairs playing cards around a small table.

Thais stops. 'Let's just sit here,' she says, lowering herself onto a bench inside the walkway.

Carolyn grips her wallet tightly and sits down. 'Where the heck are we?'

'You see this place here?' Thais says, leaning over Carolyn to point down. 'The one with the wall painting?'

Carolyn narrows her eyes and follows the line of Thais' finger to see a home covered in graffiti. She smiles to herself, recollecting all the times she's tagged walls in her hometown. She remembers the nervous wait until dark, the navigation of reaching tricky places, the sound of the can clicking as it's shaken, the smell of paint showering the concrete. 'Yeah, I see it,' Carolyn says, the scent of vanilla teasing her nose as Thais lowers her arm.

'This is a favela. And that was my home.'

'Oh.' Carolyn struggles to find the right words. 'What was it like to live there?'

'Very poor. We had nothing. My *pai* lost his job, so him and my mother had to move there, and then they had me. After many years of *Pai* trying so hard for work, my mother's family moved her back to Japan. I only get some postcards.'

'Crap, I'm sorry,' Carolyn says, feeling the intensity

of Thais' story adding weight to her own. 'But you don't live there now?'

'No. *Pai* got a job fixing the roads. And if I get sponsorship or prize money, I help pay. Now we live in a flat on the outside of Copacabana. I sleep in the bedroom and he is on the sofa.'

Carolyn doesn't speak. Thais' words cut right through her chest and nestle into the throb of her heart. For the first time in her life, Carolyn can relate to someone. She wants to explode with stories about her own life, but fear of opening up keeps the words from escaping.

'What about you?' Thais asks, taking a muesli bar from her pocket and offering half to Carolyn. 'You are best friends with the other two, but I can tell you are very different to them.'

An intensity lingers around them. Carolyn swallows and inhales a swift bolt of air that jets straight into her belly. She can feel Thais waiting patiently beside her, as if she'd wait all night for an answer if that's what it took. 'Yeah, I, err, I …' She releases a sigh. 'I guess you could say I'm poor too. I live as a house-o.'

The confusion on Thais' face prompts Carolyn to explain.

'Sorry, housing commission. Me and Mum live in

this complex that the government owns. We have to pay 'em rent, but it's a bit cheaper than normal places.'

'Wow, the government at least helps you with this. Our government is corrupt, you cannot trust. They only have interest in making money for themselves and their rich associates. It is very crap.' Thais tightens her lips and shakes her head angrily.

'Are you on the full junior tour?' Carolyn asks. 'I haven't seen you at the other comps.'

'No. I cannot afford. For now, I just do Brazil and some other small events in Peru and Chile. Then we see if I win money to do more. Are you on the tour?'

Carolyn leans on the bench. 'Yeah, I'm on the tour. I have a scholarship grant from my school.' She leaves it at that for now. It's too complicated to explain the rest: the grant running out, her friends raising money for her, the mystery cheque, the fact that every day Carolyn expects it all to be whipped away from her. She knows she could tell Thais these things, though, and that she would understand. Never before has she felt so connected to somebody.

'Do you see your mum?' Carolyn asks.

Thais absently scratches the tattoo etched on her left forearm. It's no larger than a packet of chewing gum, but Carolyn can make out the word 'Yuki'. She wonders if that's Thais' mother's name.

Thais looks away and huffs. 'Never. She has another family in Japan now. She won't be back.'

'Oh, sorry.' Carolyn decides that's enough questions. She doesn't want Thais to ask about her father. That story is too murky, like a shore break full of seaweed. Plus, this whole talking-about-your-feelings stuff is tiring.

She stifles a yawn. 'We should probably get going so I don't get busted.'

* * *

'Okay, so it was a long walkway, undercover, but mostly glass so you could see everything around you?' Mel says, whispering into the darkness.

'Yeah, but you can't see into the tunnel from the outside,' Carolyn says, her head heavy on her pillow. She barely has the energy to keep her eyes open, let alone for this interrogation about her impromptu visit to the favela. 'There's some kind of mirrored stuff on the outside.'

Jaspa is sitting up in her bed, leaning against the wall and plaiting her hair over one shoulder. 'I'm confused. Why was the tunnel there?'

'For the tourists of this fancy hotel to see the favela,' Carolyn mumbles.

'Wait.' Mel props herself up on one elbow. 'It's so the rich people can watch the poor people from the safety of a tunnel?'

'Err, yeah, I guess,' Carolyn says.

'That is so freakin' wrong on so many levels,' Mel spits.

'Shh,' Jaspa says. 'You'll wake Mum and Dad.'

'It's like a favela zoo,' Mel continues. 'A putrid display of privilege at the expense of the less fortunate. I seriously want to vomit.'

Carolyn shrugs in the dark. She hasn't thought of it like that. If anything, she feels more connected to what she saw from the tunnel than to the tourists who use it for amusement. 'We did see a robbery,' she adds sleepily. 'Right in front of us.'

Jaspa gasps, and Mel sits upright. 'What the heck?'

'Yeah, fully. Thais said it's pretty common; the favelas don't have cops. A guy walked past another guy, then walked back past him again and snatched the wallet outta his back pocket, then bolted.' It's not the first time Carolyn's seen thieves in action. The crew of guys who live in the shack next to her apartment block are forever doing dodgy acts, sometimes in full daylight for all to see, even if you don't want to.

'I can't believe Thais grew up there,' Jaspa says, finishing her plait and sliding down under the covers.

'It's so hectic, such a world away from our reality,' Mel says.

Maybe for you, Carolyn thinks. She rolls over and surrenders to sleep.

#16

Carolyn wrestles with her backpack, trying to untwist the straps so she can slip her arms through them. While she envies the ease of her friends' wheelie suitcases, when it comes to stairs she's thankful for her choice of luggage. Well, more luck than choice, given she scored it for free from a neighbour's hard rubbish. The zipper on one pocket is broken, but other than that, it's perfect.

After an early rise, a thirty-minute plane ride from Rio to Florianopolis and a one-hour shuttle, they've finally arrived at their hotel in Praia do Rosa.

'You little smartarse,' Mel calls to Carolyn, who walks effortlessly up the stairs while Mel and Jaspa clunk their cases up behind her.

'It might not be pretty, but it's functional,' Carolyn says, tugging on her backpack. 'A bit like me, really.'

Mel scoffs. 'That's quite funny, good one. But also, shut up, cos it's not true.'

'Are we there yet?' Jaspa pants.

'I reckon we are,' Carolyn says. 'I can hear your mum and dad just up ahead.' She waits for Mel and Jaspa at the top of the stairs, then they walk into the garden area together. A scattering of two-storey wooden huts sit behind a big sign that says La Playa Resort. The huts are arranged around a large, sandstone-tiled pool lined with white sunlounges, some littered with striped towels and guests' belongings. Beyond the huts sit clusters of palm trees and dense planting that dips in places to allow views of the ocean that sparkles beyond.

The world's best junior surfers chatter excitedly as their national team leaders settle them in to their home for the next four days. Carolyn spies Ellen Ryder waving to them from the bottom veranda of one of the beach-facing cabanas.

'Hi girls,' Ellen says, adjusting her floppy sunhat as Carolyn, Mel and Jaspa crunch up the short stony path to reach her. 'Isn't this just a divine little hut?'

'It kinda looks like your place, Mrs Ryder,' Carolyn says, taking in the brown wooden panels and wrap-around balcony.

'It does too,' Jaspa says, collapsing the handle of her pink and grey case and carrying it through the doorway. 'I suddenly don't feel homesick anymore. Mum, Dad, Tyler, Cooper and you girls are all here, and now we're in a house that's just like home. Winning!'

Carolyn steps inside and looks up at the exposed wooden beams that stretch across the roof, broken up by a set of stairs leading to the top level. She unclips her backpack and drops it onto the tropical printed cushions of the cane lounge. She too feels strangely at home, like she's almost connected to this place, even though she's never been here before.

'Alrighty, troops, gather round,' Anthony says as he comes down the stairs wiping sweat from his forehead with the bottom of his T-shirt. Cooper and Tyler follow closely behind him. 'Ellen and I are in the upstairs room, so let's use the diplomatic coin toss to see who nabs the other one and who'll be downstairs.'

Carolyn huffs out a small laugh. She loves how quirky Jaspa's parents are, particularly Anthony's little ritual of using a coin toss to make decisions, usually as a way to ward against Tyler's sense of entitlement.

Anthony polishes the coin against his boardshorts, which seem to be creeping higher up to his waist with each passing year. 'Who's calling?'

'Yep,' Tyler says, his hands on his hips.

'Yo, I will,' Carolyn says, half raising a hand.

'Go chick, bring this puppy home,' Mel says, slapping Carolyn on the back.

'We ready?' Anthony says, kissing the sharp edge of the fifty-cent coin and twirling it between his fingers.

'Ready,' everyone choruses.

'Tails,' Tyler shouts.

'Heads then,' Carolyn says, happy with that outcome. Heads is about leading the way, being strong. Tails feels lame, like you're following the path of others.

Anthony sends the coin spiralling into the air like an Olympic diver. Seven sets of eyes follow the coin's flight. Anthony smoothly catches the coin and whacks it onto the back of his other hand, concealing the outcome.

'Ready?' he teases.

He releases his hands and a squeal erupts from the three girls as the Queen's head appears, sitting triumphant until it's knocked away by Tyler.

'In your *face*,' Mel says, with no intention of softening the blow.

'Okay, that's enough,' Anthony says, picking the coin up off the floor and pocketing it. 'Girls, run upstairs and see how big a win your room is.'

Mel playfully pushes Carolyn towards the stairs, and

they flick off their thongs and race up to the next level. Carolyn glances to the right and sees Mr and Mrs Ryder's suitcases in the room overlooking the pool. Mel brushes past her and bolts into the room to her left.

'Oh my fricken' god!' Mel calls out.

Carolyn follows her into the room and is immediately greeted with unobstructed views of Praia do Rosa beach. There are various sections of whitewater peppered from north to south, indicating a smorgasbord of rideable banks. Three single beds made up with matching turquoise linen face the balcony, which means Carolyn will wake up to this view every morning.

'Even the beach looks like home,' Jaspa squeals with a clap of her hands.

Carolyn leans against the wooden balcony and looks over the shrub between them and the sand. Much like Bonita Shores, the beach is bookended by lush, green north and south headlands. It's another reminder of why Carolyn will do everything she can to stay on the tour. This home, this bedroom, this location, Anthony and Ellen's generosity, it's as far removed from her home life as anything could get, and she doesn't want it to be whipped away.

She hears the familiar sound of leg-ropes tapping against fibreglass. Three surfers come into view below.

'Hey!' she calls down.

Thais stops and looks up. 'Oh, *olá amiga*. You guys, come surfing!'

'Okay. Does that track lead to the beach?'

'*Sim*,' Thais says, adjusting the surfboard under her arm as her two teammates walk on ahead. 'It leads to mid Rosa. Today is strong south wind, so we go south end, more protected.'

Carolyn gives Thais a wave as she disappears along the track into the bushes. She turns to Mel and Jaspa, who are busy checking out the adjacent bathroom. 'Hey, let's see if your dad or Mr Sampson can take us surfing, I'm frothin' to get in the water.'

'Girls,' Anthony yells from downstairs with impeccable timing. 'Grab your stuff, we're going to hit the waves.'

Carolyn is already wearing her boardshorts, so she heads downstairs, whips off her T-shirt to expose her cross-back bikini top, fishes her long-sleeved wetsuit vest out of her backpack and slips it on. Outside in the garden, Anthony has removed everyone's surfboards from the travel bags and is working on screwing in the fins.

'Oh, who brought these up for us?' Carolyn asks as she bends down to help.

'One of the hotel staff, Renato, helped me.'

Anthony points to a young man carrying two sets of surfboard bags to one of the other cabins. 'He's a good guy. Left an accountant career in the city to live the relaxed surfer life out here.'

'I can see why,' says Carolyn, turning her fin key to tighten the last screw, then flipping her board over to rub a block of wax over the deck. 'It's beautiful.'

The familiar honey scent of the wax triggers a wave of anticipation. It feels like forever since she's connected with the sea. The surf they had in Rio was more frustrating than fun. She's eager to get to know this break they've been watching from the balcony, and also Thais. Every conversation they have offers a perspective that would never have otherwise entered Carolyn's thoughts. She's used to the dynamic with her two best friends, where Mel is the one with the busy brain and Jaspa the deep thinker while Carolyn simply trails behind, just getting by. It's like trying to paddle out through a ferocious shore break when the groundswell just keeps forcing her back: she never gives up.

'Alright gang,' Anthony shouts through the open front door. 'The boards are prepped, let's go.'

Tyler and Cooper are the first to collect their boards. 'Dad, can we just meet you out there?' says Tyler. 'The girls are lagging.'

'Sure, *vai*, but stick to the track. We'll be there in a sec.'

'We're going to the south end,' Carolyn adds. 'Carn chicks, hurry up!' she calls, standing at the door with her board tucked under her arm, ready to go.

Mel and Jaspa thump down the stairs with thunderous footsteps. 'Sorry,' Mel says, jumping the last couple of steps. 'Jaspa had a bikini disaster that required some serious strategic thinking and the precision of my masterful hands,' Mel says, wiggling her fingers in the air.

'Hair caught in the back buckle,' Jaspa clarifies with a smile, twisting her hair up and securing it with a band.

'C'mon, let's hit it,' Carolyn says, drumming her fingers on the side of her board. 'The boys have already bolted.'

The three girls follow Anthony to the bushes where the track begins. Although they're on the other side of the world, this could easily be mistaken for somewhere in Australia. They reach the beach to see Tyler and Cooper already sharing a right-hander, riding towards them. Cooper is in front in a widened goofy stance, racing along the top of the wave to keep ahead of Tyler, who remains close to the pocket of foam, climbing it each time it breaks.

'C'mon, can't let them have all the fun,' Mel says, breaking into a jog.

The water is cooler than Rio, and Carolyn is glad she's wearing a wetsuit top. They push off the sand into the rip that runs against the rocks, allowing it to carry them out into the line-up. Carolyn looks towards the beach and can just make out their balcony. Jaspa's bright pink towel hanging over the rails makes for the perfect landmark. Several other surfers emerge from the bushy track out onto the beach, and Carolyn to feels a sense of urgency as she waits for her first wave. While being on the junior tour is fun, it also means there's an instant crowd of frothers wherever they go.

She hears someone yell 'go' from down the line, and sees Thais sitting upright and cupping her hands to her mouth. A peak picks Carolyn up, leaving her only a second to position her feet onto her board mid-air. She lands with a thump at the bottom of the wave with too much weight on her back foot, and her hips swivel awkwardly. Her surfboard catapults from under her feet, and she lands with a slap, back-first against the water.

Carolyn gathers her board and paddles back out.

'Ouch,' Thais says. 'Maybe it was wrong I call you into that one.'

'Nah, it's just me,' Carolyn says, tugging her rash

vest back down. 'The long plane trip, then the crappy surf in Rio. I just feel like a bit of a gumby.'

'What is gummy?'

'Gumby,' Carolyn says. 'Like a kook.'

'Oh, I know kook.' Thais laughs. 'I think this one is same in Brazil.'

'Yep, well, I'd be the dictionary definition today.' Carolyn clenches her teeth. She can't be in a world junior event and fall off like that. She already feels like enough of a phony.

'I think you have big doubts on yourself,' Thais says, squinting her eyes against the sun. 'I don't know why.'

A surge of water rolls towards Carolyn, saving her from having to respond. She doesn't want to waste words talking about herself. She's sure people will get bored before she's even had a chance to begin.

As the ocean stirs beneath her and Carolyn strokes through the water, she feels the familiar swirl she gets in her tummy when the wave is just about to break. Her palms press onto the fibreglass and her core strength guides her, both feet landing effortlessly on the deck. *This is more like it,* she thinks, leaning into a bottom turn so beautifully drawn out, it's a wonder she can achieve such grace on a high-performance shortboard. *Grace.* That's not usually a word used to describe Carolyn's surfing. Commentators have thrown around terms like power, pocket rocket and solid, but never graceful. Carolyn can feel something stirring within her, a transformation, perhaps. The only trouble is, she can't quite put her finger on what it is yet.

#17

'This is the view of Rosa from our balcs. Rosa is what the locals call it, and today is day one of competition, so let's hope it's pumping.'

Mel is walking around the bedroom in her star-patterned pyjamas, holding her phone above her head to film a live video. As the sun creeps into view to signal the arrival of morning, a wisp of cloud acts as a veil, creating splotches of purple and orange against an otherwise hazy blue sky.

'Here we have Carolyn.' Mel steps up onto the end of Carolyn's bed and flips her phone around from the selfie position. 'So, Carolyn, tell us what your competitive strategy will be today.'

'Huh?' Carolyn stirs awake and rolls onto her back, rubbing her eyes. 'What are you doing, ya psycho?'

'Tell the world what a kick-ass surfer you are. Go on.'

Carolyn looks through bleary eyes at the screen that's pointed at her face. 'I'm a kook who somehow has bluffed my way on the tour. There, satisfied?' She rolls back to face the wall and pulls the sheet up over her head.

Mel sighs and stops recording. 'No, I am not.' She hops off the bed and speaks to Carolyn's back. 'You know, Carolyn, we all believe in your ability. It's just a shame that you don't. I'll see you downstairs. Breakfast is ready and we have to leave for the beach in halfa.'

The change in Mel's tone renders Carolyn fully awake; it's like having a bucket of icy water thrown over her. She stares wide-eyed at the wall as her tummy does somersaults. Nerves about the competition or anxiety about how others perceive her? She doesn't like unpacking her feelings; they tend to stay stuffed into little corners, growing mould until something triggers their unearthing.

Bursts of laughter drift upstairs from the kitchen. Sometimes light-heartedness helps her out of a slump, but sometimes she finds it stifling. Having darkness around can sometimes act as permission to wallow in her own. Even more confusingly, some-times that very permission to feel dark is all it takes to flip her onto that bright side that everybody bangs on about.

She takes a deep breath and rolls onto her back, then kicks off the sheet and walks over to the balcony. The sun has risen enough to reveal the lines of swell that are etched across the ocean, like it's been perfectly drawn by hand. Carolyn can spot at least two different breaking peaks through sections of bushland. She pictures herself wearing a competition vest, riding the waves all the way to the shore.

'Carolyn,' Ellen calls from downstairs. 'You up, honey?'

'Coming,' Carolyn calls back. Mrs Ryder's chipper and understanding voice suddenly makes her feel guilty about her own sombre mood. *Today's going to be a good day,* she thinks as she slips into her boardshorts. She makes a conscious effort to lighten her step as she walks downstairs.

'Here she is, our little ray of light,' Anthony says genuinely, holding a tray of fried eggs, mushrooms and toast. 'Sit down, love. You've got the choice of my trademark fry-up, or fruit, muesli and yoghurt.'

'You know I can't resist your fry-up, Mr Ryder. Load me up.' Carolyn grabs a piece of toast, an egg and a spoonful of mushrooms from the tray, and a slice of avocado from the table. It's only a fraction of what she'd usually eat, but competing on a full stomach is a rookie error she only made once – one that resulted in a mid-heat ocean vomit and a fourth placing.

She looks across the table at Jaspa and Mel, who are giggling together, even though they've drawn each other for their very first heat. Carolyn wonders how long it'll be before Mel flicks the switch to put point scores before friendship. Sometimes it happens prior to paddling out, sometimes it doesn't happen at all unless Mel is losing the heat. Up until now, they've been lucky this year, and have managed to avoid being on the same side of the draw.

Carolyn begins to clear the table, scraping the plates and then stacking them.

'Don't worry about that, darling,' Ellen says from the kitchen. 'Flavia will clean up.'

'Flavia?' Carolyn asks.

'Yes, the villas come with a maid. Flavia will help us cook and clean; you can just concentrate on competing. Run upstairs with the girls and get your stuff together.'

Carolyn can't keep herself from at least taking the pile of dishes into the kitchen and placing them on the sink. 'Okay, will do. Thanks, Mrs Ryder.'

'Hey, did you know we have a maid?' Carolyn asks the girls when she reaches the bedroom. 'Like, that means no doing the dishes and no making our bed for almost a week.' While most kids are coerced into doing these chores by the promise of pocket money, for Carolyn it's always been an unpaid chore she's surrendered to, simply to avoid living in a pigsty.

'We know,' Mel says, throwing items from her suitcase into her beach bag one at a time. 'It leaves us more time to dominate the competition and find hotties to hook up with.'

Carolyn looks at Jaspa and Jaspa smiles back at her. Mel seems to have forgotten that Jaspa's in the same heat as her, and that she already has a boyfriend.

'Ready girls?' Anthony calls from downstairs.

'Coming, Dad,' Jaspa replies, slipping into her favourite floral bralette and hipster pant bikinis, then putting on her three-quarter sleeve Spell playsuit.

'Terrible choice for a sneaky beach bush wee,' Mel says, pointing at Jaspa's outfit.

'Why?' Jaspa asks innocently.

'You'll see,' Mel says, winking at Carolyn as they walk downstairs. 'Just don't wait til it's urgent, or Flavia will be doing way more washing than she's paid for.'

They collect their surfboards and follow the other junior surfers down the track to the beach, the chatter a cacophony of different languages and accents. Tents line the beach with signage advertising sponsors, most of whom Carolyn has never heard of before. She guesses they're local Brazilian companies and wonders what they sell.

A commentator tests the microphone as Tones and I pumps out over the speaker. Carolyn's heard this song nearly every day she's been in Brazil; at the hotel in Rio, in the shops at the airport, on the radio. She can't believe this artist from Byron Bay, not far from where she lives, is being celebrated all the way over here in Brazil. Carolyn is constantly looking up her interviews because she loves the way the artist talks about believing in herself and carving her own path, and how being a good person should matter more than what you look like.

They reach the tent where the rest of the Australian team have spread out their gear and set up their towels, all singing in unison.

'Can you believe they're playing this at the beach?' Mel squeals, dancing with her surfboard tucked under her arm. 'It feels just like home.'

Even the man testing the microphone joins in, singing the lyrics with a Brazilian accent.

Carolyn slips out of her day pack and wedges the nose of her surfboard into the sand, no longer embarrassed by the dings, the yellowing fibreglass and the lack of sponsor stickers. That's all thanks to her boss, who provided her with three new boards and a sponsorship package of $2000 worth of wetsuits, swimwear and clothing for the year, as well as paying her wages. That's another thing that the Tones and I singer always says: she couldn't do what she does without the support of those who care about her. Carolyn feels the same way; it's just not her family who offer the support.

'Okay, team,' Thomas claps, bringing the Australians to attention. 'Let's get into some warm-ups. The girls will run first. Carolyn, you're second heat.'

Carolyn nods, then takes position at the back of the group to follow Thomas's sequence of stretches and squats, ending on a round of twenty burpees. She's extra thankful she resisted a second helping of breakfast, vowing to try and get up earlier next time so her food has more time to settle.

The siren blares over the loudspeaker to mark the start of heat one, so Carolyn walks across the sand to collect her rashie. She's in blue, which she's happy with. As well as being the colour of her favourite footy team, it's better than pink or green. She returns to her board and gives it another coating of wax, not necessarily for added grip – more like added confidence. The criss-crossing movement helps calm her nerves. If she can make it through this heat, she'll be one step closer to winning some prize money.

She slips into the blue vest. She's the first competitor

to wear it today, so it's crispy dry and warm against her skin. As luck will have it, it also pairs perfectly with her brown and blue-striped boardshorts, a Christmas gift from Jaspa. Bikini bottoms are great for freedom of movement, but they make Carolyn feel way too exposed in front of a beach full of people, and besides, she hates seeing her butt hang out in event photography.

'That left has your name scrawled all over it,' Mel says, picking up Carolyn's leg-rope and pulling fluff from the Velcro strap.

Carolyn looks at the ocean and sees a wave holding up, pressing against the undercurrents and providing her with a blank canvas to mentally surf on in preparation for her heat.

'Yeah, I reckon you're right,' Carolyn says, accepting the leg-rope from Mel. 'Here goes nothin'.'

Cheers from the Australian team echo like a flock of cockatoos as Carolyn walks across the sand. It's another nice reminder of home. Mel always jokes about how cockatoos sound so Aussie bogan.

She bends down to attach her leg-rope to her ankle and sees the three other competitors in her peripheral vision. Girls from Hawaii, France and Brazil are in her heat and they all have sponsor's stickers on their boards. It's amazing how a piece of adhesive can carry such weight. Carolyn stands her board upright and rubs her hand over the logo of the surf shop, wondering if she deserves its placement or if it's a pity offering.

'Heat one, you have five minutes remaining. Surfers in heat two you can now paddle out,' announces the commentator.

Carolyn runs through the shallows, launches her board over the whitewater and lands on it belly first. She adjusts her hips so they slip into the slight indents they've made in the fibreglass, and paddles strongly into position.

The other surfers in the heat are natural footers and favour the right-hander, while Carolyn drifts over to the left. With no other surfer present to mark the best take-off spot, she monitors the ocean, waiting for the hooter to sound. The wave is breaking before it reaches her, but hits a sketchy section that seems to close out on every other wave. If she sits on this side of that section she can use the power of the broken water to ride the remaining two thirds of the wave. The bigger five-foot sets are holding up really wide, at least 20 metres from where she's sitting, but they're infrequent and unpredictable. She decides to stay put and make the most of what she has, right here, right now.

While the other three surfers hassle each other for waves, Carolyn goes unnoticed. Perhaps that's the advantage of having a surfboard void of major sponsor stickers. When she surfs her backhand it's more of a power play, using the weight of her back foot to force aggression into her top turns. But when she's on her forehand, like now on the lefts, it's like a dance with nature, aided by the Tones and I song that remains wormed into her ear for the entire heat.

No one's there to hassle Carolyn out of waves. She's all alone on this big, blue dance floor. Pushing her board to the sky in frontside snaps, leaning into the rail for foam-bouncing cutbacks and busting out the rounded-square tail of her board for wave-completing manoeuvres. As she paddles back out with time for only one more ride, she spies a line bigger than she's seen all heat creeping towards the wide bank. She stops paddling, willing to gamble that this is the ride she's been hoping for. She straddles her board and swirls her legs and hands through the water to hold herself in position. The wave rises as an invitation to dance, and the chorus of the song rings through her ears as she glides into a wave almost double her height.

The open wall of water in front of her requires a different style of surfing than the previous waves. She draws big, deep lines to bookmark where she's been, and each section allows her to play with a variety of turns as the spectators roar their support from the beach. She commits to a close-out shore break with a dynamic float across the foam, then descends into the shallows with a stomach-dropping sensation. The siren sounds and she exits the water with no idea of the scores, until Mel and Jaspa bolt over, hooting and grinning widely.

Jaspa takes Carolyn's board and tucks it under her arm. 'You surfed incredible! And you had the left all to yourself.'

'I know, I guess they didn't see me as a threat.'

Mel passes Carolyn her drink bottle. 'They were all scrapping over on the right. The chick from Hawaii came second.'

'Were did I come?' Carolyn asks, taking a big swig of water and realising she's hungry again.

'You won, you goose,' Mel blurts, shoving Carolyn in the arm then grabbing her by the rash vest to stop her from toppling over.

'I did? Oh rad. I honestly had no idea, I was just surfing my brains out.' She smiles to herself, thinking maybe, after all, it's not the sticker on your board that matters, it's the way you ride it.

#18

Carolyn wishes Mel and Jaspa good luck as they break away to prepare for their heat. She's thankful she didn't have to compete against one of them. The last time she drew Jaspa was a month ago on the New South Wales Central Coast. It was the second round, and instead of playing tactics like they should have been, they took turns going wave-for-wave. With four minutes remaining, Jaspa nabbed a set wave that tunnelled perfectly around her, like she was skating through an overhead drainpipe. Carolyn waited for her turn, but it never came, and she ended up in third place, knocking her out of the competition. Jaspa apologised so much that Carolyn had to suppress her annoyance. For Carolyn, a loss is more than just a dent to her ego. Jaspa knows this, so the result cut her up.

The sand forms a crust on Carolyn's damp feet and the mid-morning sun offsets the coolness of the offshore breeze. She stops and holds her board between her legs, pinching it with her knees, as she peels off her competition rash vest and returns it to the officials. The young woman behind the desk congratulates her, noting that Carolyn's last ride earned her nine points. Carolyn smiles, awkwardly accepting of the compliment, then retreats before anyone expects her to say something.

Mel and Jaspa will be paddling out soon, so Carolyn heads towards the tent to watch them with her team-mates. As she does, something catches her eye. She stops short, and a coolness trickles through her body. Surely, she must be imagining it? She hesitates a while longer, then averts her eyes. It's difficult to tell, as this man is wearing sunglasses, but she feels like he's staring at her.

Is this the same guy who creeped her out at the hotel restaurant in Rio? He's standing a few feet in front of her bag, so she changes course and walks down to the shoreline. She sits on the sand next to her surfboard and tries to keep her imagination under control. The man looks like a surfer; his wide shoulders and solid, confident stance gives it away. Maybe he's an old-school Brazilian surfer that Carolyn's seen in her boss's stack of vintage *Salt Action* magazines? Maybe it's not *him* staring at *Carolyn*, but her recognising him.

She pours sand through her fingers as doubts dart about in her head. She could tell Anthony and Ellen about it, but what's there to tell? And isn't it enough of a burden that they have to look after her like she's their own daughter? They're here for a holiday. She doesn't want to ruin that with unnecessary drama.

She looks up at the line-up and sees that the heat has started. Mel and Jaspa are both in position to score a ride as a wave pops up underneath them and splits in two directions. Jaspa takes the left on her backhand and Mel the right. Their styles are completely different; Jaspa is flawlessly fluid, which is sometimes misread as being too relaxed on the wave, while Mel is fast, whippy and dynamic. Jaspa falls before completing her ride, having lost focus and been bucked off the wave as it collided with an outgoing rip. But Mel meets the end section of her wave and slices her rail through the water like a knife through a cucumber. Mel gets the better of the exchange, being awarded an 8.3, while Jaspa's fall gains her a 4.7. Carolyn hopes that Huey will offer her two friends this kind of diplomacy for the entire heat; split peaks that lessen the need for gameplay.

'Why you sit alone?' says a familiar voice from behind her. Thais throws a towel down next to her and then bends down to place another over Carolyn's shoulders. 'I thought you might need this. The sun, the wind, it can burn.' She rests her hands in the grooves of Carolyn's shoulders, leaning on them as she lowers herself to the sand.

'Thanks,' Carolyn says, avoiding Thais' question. She could tell her about the staring man, ask her opinion, but decides it's easier to shove it into the corner of her mind, where all her secrets and fears gather dust. 'My two friends are surfing against each other.'

'You think they are better than you, yes?'

Whoa, what, where did that come from? 'No,' she jumps in, then hesitates. 'Well, yes. I dunno.' Her body language encourages silence. *Don't start this crap.* Just because Thais has detected some cracks in Carolyn's veneer doesn't mean it's okay for her to start chipping away at them.

'I saw you surf, and I see them surf. You are just as good,' Thais says. Her delivery is like a rocky road, a combination of both hard and soft.

'Whatever.' Carolyn picks up a clump of seaweed next to her and starts popping the bobbles. She's torn between not wanting to unveil too much of herself, but appreciating being asked. Each piece of seaweed rolls between her thumb and forefinger, its tightness relieved by combustion under Carolyn's command.

Thais moves her hand to rest next to Carolyn's and also picks off seaweed bobbles. They take turns popping them as they watch the heat draw to a close. 'I think your friend Mel is going to win this one,' Thais says, staring straight ahead from beneath her sunglasses.

'I reckon you're right,' Carolyn says, moving her hand away to draw both knees up to her chest. 'She's an amazing competitor. She's great at knowing what she wants and going for it.'

'Are you?'

'Am I what?'

'Are you good at knowing what you want and going for it?'

'Not so much, I guess.'

'I think you should stop feeling like only you are lucky to have your friends.'

Carolyn stiffens. 'But why? I am lucky.'

'Yes. But they are also lucky to have you. And that is what you don't believe.'

'Oh.' Carolyn has never considered it a privilege for anyone else to be in her company. Ever.

She watches Mel and Jaspa meet in the shallows and exit the water after their heat. They stop for a moment as Jaspa wraps her arms around Mel and draws her in close, making sure the thirty-minute rivalry doesn't follow them out onto the sand.

'I feel greetful to meet you,' Thais says, as they both stand and brush off the sand.

'Dude, you're getting a bit freakin' deep there,' Carolyn says, grappling for the bricks to build up a wall, but amused at Thais' use of incorrect vowels.

'I know, but deep is where all the magic happens.'

'Magic?'

'*Sim*, magic. You'll see.'

Carolyn shrugs and looks back to see that the man has left. 'I'd better go and check in with my team and get ready for the quarters.'

'Yes, me too. I'm in the first one.'

They stand in silence for a moment as the activity of the event – the people, the commentary, the sound of the crashing waves – swarms around them.

'Oh, this is yours,' Carolyn says, removing the towel from around her shoulders. 'Thanks.'

'Thank you, Carolyn. For this,' Thais says, holding up the towel, 'and for sharing your time.'

'Errr, okay, you're welcome.'

Thais leaves and Carolyn walks up the beach, the sun penetrating her skin, her top half now only covered in a bikini top. She feels a sense of freedom at being so exposed.

#19

'Surfers in quarter final number four, you have fifteen minutes remaining,' the commentator's voice echoes through the loudspeaker.

Carolyn sits on her surfboard, drumming her hands on the deck and rocking with the movement of the swell. The changing tide has meant the competitors have shifted to a different bank, slightly north of where they were this morning. Mel was knocked out of the first quarter final, leaving only two Australian females in the competition. Carolyn looks over at Tara Watson, who's staying in the cabana next to them. She yawns, and Carolyn figures all that sneaking out to party with the other teams has probably caught up with her. It's definitely been a topic of conversation at this year's tour.

Her nickname, Chapstick, is directly related to the number of guys she's kissed.

Carolyn wonders if Tara knows she's been branded this way. Carolyn chooses to hover on the outer boundaries of bitchiness. She doesn't instigate it, and tries her hardest not to feed it, but she doesn't stand up to it, either. That would require courage and energy that she doesn't have.

Junco Ogawa, a softly-spoken Japanese competitor, paddles for the same wave as Tara. Carolyn is surprised to see Junco hold her ground against the dominant Australian and glide into an overhead ride. Carolyn is fascinated by how light and fluid the Japanese surfers on the tour are. Everything they do seems effortless. Their take-offs make them look like falling leaves, their turns like ballerinas. Japan has embraced Junco as their next rising star and Carolyn's seen Instagram pics showing her on billboards and teen magazine covers. She's even had a takeaway sushi roll named after her.

Tara thumps her fist through the water in frustration as she sees Junco zoom all the way to the beach like a wind-up surfer toy. Carolyn looks down at her watch to see that the screen is foggy. 'Crap,' she whispers, shaking her wrist in the hope that it's just a temporary malfunction. But still no digits are visible. She needs to know the scores and how much time remains. She was sitting in second position, which would push her through to the semi finals, but with Junco's ride and the American surfer with the blonde plaits also posting scores, Carolyn's not sure how hard she'll have to fight to remain in the top two. She raises her wrist in the air and taps it, prompting the commentators to give them an update, then waits.

The rising onshore wind has chopped up the waves, making it difficult to select the best rides. Carolyn swivels her legs underneath her board to keep herself in position, the water now so murky she can barely see past her feet. When she lets herself think about the fact that she's surfing in a completely different ocean, the thought unsettles her. What lies beneath her? Do they even have sharks in Brazil? The increasing current tries to pull her off the break and her hands stroke into the water one at a time to fight against it. In surfing, there are so many elements to battle just to get a wave. It's a bit like her life, Carolyn thinks.

The commentators announce that there are five minutes remaining. Carolyn is in third place. She needs a 6.3 to progress into second and an 8.4 to move into first. Carolyn, Mel and Jaspa each approach competitive surfing with a different mindset. Mel harnesses any nerves to fill herself with even more confidence. She has uncontested faith in her own ability, and is sure she'll one day be celebrated as a world champion. Jaspa has a carefree approach to surfing, trusting that the ocean will provide her with what's meant to be. She gets more satisfaction from measuring her performance against herself rather than against others. Carolyn, on the other hand, is often crippled by imposter syndrome. A poor score solidifies her belief that she doesn't deserve to be a competitive surfer. She doesn't go out there to win, she goes out there and attempts to delay what she's sure is an inevitable loss. Everyone else funds themselves or is the right marketing fit for a sponsor to support them. Carolyn's financial start came from a government grant. Should that really entitle her to a place on a world surfing tour?

Six points is more than achievable for Carolyn. Her highest score this heat so far was an 8.1. Her lowest was a two, but that's because her back foot slipped out on a bottom turn and slapped her stomach-first onto the wave.

A lump of water offers itself to her, but as Carolyn begins to paddle she sees it has the potential to close out, so she quickly yanks her board back to wait for a better ride.

Just then, she hears a loud sharp whistle from the beach and looks up to see a figure waving their arms, furiously pointing south, to Carolyn's left. She looks north and sees that the other surfers are some distance from her, hassling each other for a wave, so the person must be gesturing to her. They continue to whistle frantically, encouraging her down the beach.

A moment later she sees a line of swell rising from the flats, producing the biggest set of the day. The other competitors are too far out of position to catch it; she may not even make it in time herself. But the person on the beach seems to think she will; their whistle carries over the sound of the ocean, ringing through her ears.

She swivels her board south and uses her feet to push through the water, propelling herself into a scrambling paddle towards the forming peak. The ideal take-off point is another two strokes away, but she risks the ride running away from her if she waits that long. Running on pure instinct, she points her surfboard to shore and quickly rises with the lip as it throws her towards the beach, where all her teammates fall silent in anticipation.

She can see the curtain of water pitching before her, threatening a clean swoop of destruction. The easy way out would be to straighten towards shore and kiss any chance of progressing into the semi final goodbye. Instead, Carolyn angles straight down the line, crouches into a low stance and slots under the wall of water falling before her. A roar from the beach unites all countries as competitors cheer on this spectacular display of surfing.

Carolyn tunnels through the moving water, struggling to believe that she not only made the drop, but also managed to backdoor into a barrel – something you can't do unless you have 100 per cent confidence in yourself. The sound of crashing foam echoes from behind her, encouraging her to continue the race away from it, and the light from the setting sun ahead of her beckons her out into the open. With very little tube riding experience, pure instinct is what guides her to avoid the end section of the wave and exit into the shore break, somehow managing to remain standing.

The ocean collides behind her and she cups both hands over her head and throws it back in disbelief at what she just experienced. She reaches the shallows and sinks, still standing on her board, realising that she not only just scored the wave of her life, but did so in a competition. Mel and Jaspa race down the beach with hoots of joy, straight past the person who helped Carolyn just win the quarter final.

And that's when Carolyn realises that the suspicion that she was being followed wasn't just her imagination. Because there he is.

20

'You little ninja, I can't believe you backdoored that nugget!' Mel says, roughing up Carolyn's wet curls as they walk up the beach.

'Yes, what did it feel like?' Jaspa asks. 'I've never taken off into a barrel from that far behind the peak. Was it scary?'

Carolyn sees the man walk off ahead of them to follow the Brazilian team up the bush track back towards the cabanas. Her breath shortens. She wonders if he knows them, and if he's staying at the hotel. Should she tell Mr and Mrs Ryder, or even Mr Sampson? She doesn't want to cause a drama, especially not when everything's going so perfectly. She's through to the semi final of a world tour event and is guaranteed some prize money, she's staying with her two best friends in an amazing beachfront hut in Brazil, she's even made a new friend who she's starting to open up to. Does she really need to stuff it all up by reporting this creep and causing chaos? What would she even say? *Oh, he's looking at me like a weirdo and helping me catch waves?* Everyone will think she's an idiot. Stuff that. She's only here for two more days, she'll just suck it up.

'Well, was it scary?' Jaspa repeats, placing her hand on Carolyn's surfboard.

'Huh? Oh, yeah … no. Sorry, I'm still buzzing from it all.' Carolyn regathers her thoughts. 'It's almost like taking off on a closeout and trying to get around the section, but you can see light through a small opening of the wave, so you just go for it. I just did it, I didn't really think about it.'

'Well, you knocked out Tara in the dying seconds, so that should be fun dinnertime vibes,' Mel whispers as they reach the Australian team's tent.

'Crap. Oh well, here goes,' Carolyn says as she bats away compliments about her spectacular finish.

'Carolyn!' Anthony says, bringing his hands together for one big clap. 'I can't believe you managed to spot the wide set away from the other surfers, and paddle over there so quickly. What a stroke of luck.'

'Yep, luck,' Carolyn agrees, returning a small grin to Anthony's widened smile.

'I'll just be a minute,' she says, taking off her competition vest to return it to the officials. She looks around, hoping to see Thais, but most of the teams have packed up and left the beach already, leaving only those countries who still have surfers in the fourth quarter final. She returns to Mel and Jaspa, and they pack up their belongings and follow their teammates along the bush track.

Mel yawns. 'I'm kinda tired.'

'Me too,' Carolyn says. 'And hungry.' She's gone several hours without eating anything. That must be a record.

'Hey, Dad,' Jaspa calls towards the front of the group. 'What's for dinner tonight?'

Anthony turns around and calls back, 'Flavia's made some salads, and all the teams are getting together for a traditional Brazilian barbecue. Don't worry, honey, she's got you some vegetarian.'

'Goodie, I love Flavia already,' Jaspa says, lightly clapping her hands.

As they enter the grounds of the hotel, they hear splashing, laughing and loud music. The garden area is full of surfers in boardshorts and bikinis, and the scene resembles a pool party in a Hollywood film. People are perched on each other's shoulders playing some kind of pool volleyball, while others egg each other on as they tackle a slack line that's strung between two trees.

'Look, Mel, there's your new BF,' Jaspa says as Luis whips off his T-shirt, exposing his rippled torso, and does a backflip into the pool.

'Oh, hello, it looks like tonight could get *very* interesting,' Mel says, pushing her aviator sunglasses up onto her head.

Carolyn nudges Mel with her elbow as they reach their hut to drop off their boards. 'I thought you were tired.'

Mel winks. 'Let's just say I've suddenly got a second wind.'

Carolyn puts her board in the laundry at the back of the hut, says hello to Flavia, who's busy preparing dinner in the kitchen, then goes upstairs for a quick shower. She leaves her hair salty. Washing it will make it boof out like a dandelion; she prefers it looking crusty and rugged. Footsteps thump up the stairs as Mel and Jaspa race each other to the bathroom, filling the house with screams and giggles.

'Let's just go in together,' Mel pants as they try to block each other from the door. 'It'll be heaps quicker, which leaves more time to part-ay.'

'Good thinking,' Jaspa says as they strip down to their bikinis and have a two-minute rinse. 'Are you washing your hair?' Jaspa says over the sound of the running water.

'I didn't,' Carolyn shouts back through the open bathroom door. She fishes out her denim shorts and a white shoestring strap top from her backpack and puts them on over her semi-wet skin.

'Nah, time's precious,' Mel says, hurriedly dipping her head under the shower then exiting to pat herself dry with a towel. 'Plus, you know we'll end up in the pool anyway.'

As Mel and Jaspa get changed, Carolyn takes her flannel shirt off the end of the bed and wraps it around her waist. She feels excited about tonight, though she doesn't know why. Perhaps it's because the barbecue is practically on their doorstep, so there's none of that awkwardness of having to walk into a party with people wondering what you're doing there and who invited you. Or maybe it's because of the whispers of adulation she's been hearing about her wave in the quarter final. Carolyn certainly doesn't thrive in the spotlight, but she also often struggles with feeling out of place. It's nice to be noticed for her successes, not her difference.

'Are you taking your swimmers down with you?' Jaspa asks, midway through putting on a dress.

'I've got them on underneath,' Mel says, pulling across the low neck of her T-shirt to reveal her bikini strap.

'Me too,' Carolyn says.

'Oh, good idea. I'll just be a sec.'

'Hurry up, we'll meet you in the lounge,' Mel says, tugging Carolyn out of the room. 'She'll be with Cooper all night anyway,' Mel whispers as they trot down the stairs and sit on the couch.

'So, have you spotted any hotties to home in on?' Mel asks Carolyn, out of earshot of Anthony, who walks past carrying a tray of meat, fish and vegetables for the barbecue.

'I dunno,' Carolyn says sheepishly, whacking Mel in the thigh with the back of her hand. 'That Frenchie is cute, but have you seen the chicks he hangs out with?'

'Who cares?' Mel says, coaxing Carolyn up off the couch as Jaspa joins them. 'Did those chicks air drop into the mother of all sets today and get spat through into daylight? No, they did not. You gotta own that crap.'

Carolyn shrugs and glances up at Jaspa, feeling a pang of jealousy that she can look so obliviously gorgeous with zero effort. For once, Carolyn would like to know what it's like to have a guy appreciate every part of you – the sound of your voice, the things you laugh at, the way you dress, the obscure music you like – as Cooper does with Jaspa. Carolyn's guy encounters never go beyond a quick fling, which has everything to do with her choice of guys. After all, if she goes for the hell-raising bad boys who have no interest in emotional connection, there can be no surprises or self-loathing when they don't call the next day.

The three of them walk into the garden and stop to the scene. Smoke steams from the barbecue, carrying chargrilled smells that trigger their post-surf hunger.

'I may be vegetarian, but I'll be honest, that smells delicious,' Jaspa says with her nose to the air.

'Maybe I could try to give up meat this year too,' Carolyn says with a slow nod of her head. 'You know, for the environment.'

'What? You?' Mel says, shocked. 'No freakin' way you will. The day you give up meat is the day I'll give up Brazilian hotties. Now, who's going to be my wing-woman and come and talk to Luis with me?'

'I'm going to say hi to Cooper. I've barely seen him all day and he got knocked out of the comp too,' Jaspa says.

'Party pooper. I thought you were my best friend?'

'I am your best friend, and I've been your wingwoman since you first started chasing boys at, like, eight years old.'

'Okay, true dat. Carolyn?'

Carolyn rolls her eyes. Here she goes again, third wheel incoming. 'Sure, come on.'

She follows Mel over to Luis, who is half in the water, leaning on the side of the pool talking in Portuguese to two guys.

'Hey, it's my koala,' he says, placing his hand around Mel's ankle. 'Do koalas like to swim?'

'Don't you dare,' Mel squeals, turning the cute flirt-o-meter up to eleven.

'Come on, I've been waiting all day, there's a space for you right here.' He pats the wet tiles next to him.

'Carolyn, join us?' Mel asks.

She shakes her head. 'Nah, man. You'll be right, I'm sure he'll look after you.'

Carolyn leaves Mel to strip down to her bikinis and slip into the water, then goes and sits on the bench under a thatch-roofed gazebo. She watches everyone mingling and laughing, thinking it's nice to see different cultures melding together like this.

Flavia comes over carrying a plate of food. '*Pão de queijo*, Miss Carolyn?'

'Oh, cheers, Flavia,' Carolyn says, taking a handful and biting into the bread.

'You really like the cheese bread, huh?' says a familiar voice from behind her.

Carolyn swings around with her mouth full of dough and sees Thais leaning against the pole with a smirk. Upon seeing her, Carolyn feels that instant warmth again.

'Hey, dude,' Carolyn says through the stickiness. 'You got me into them in the in the first place.'

'I know, I remember well,' Thais says, sitting on the bench next to Carolyn and drawing one knee up to her chest. 'Why you call me dude, isn't this for boys?'

'Ha,' Carolyn says, wrapping the remaining cheese ball into a napkin and placing it on the table. 'I call everyone dude. It's a bad habit, I guess.'

'Or a sweet habit,' Thais says, her skin folding into the small dimple on her right cheek.

Carolyn watches Thais' eyes soften; eyes that seem to carry so many stories and insights.

'Check this out,' Carolyn says, opening up YouTube on her phone and searching for a song. 'Jaspa's dad showed it to me. It's a bit dumb, but it's pretty funny,' she says as Scatterbrain's 'Don't Call Me Dude' blasts from the phone.

Thais pauses, listening to the lyrics and nodding her head so her dark hair flops in her face. They snicker at the weird video clip and mime the frantic guitar riff.

'I like this, I am adding it to my favourites,' Thais says, brushing a hand past Carolyn's knee and taking out her phone to save the song. 'Now I want to show you something, it's very Brazilian. Wait here.'

Thais wanders over to the barbecue and says something to Flavia in Portuguese, then returns with two plates piled with food. 'Do you have a balcony in your hut?' Thais asks.

'Yeah, upstairs. You wanna go?'

'*Sim*, we can eat up there.'

Carolyn takes one of the plates and they walk past Mel, who is close enough to Luis to be brushing against his skin, but not close enough for the adults to get suspicious. Jaspa is sitting on the front porch with Cooper and her parents, eating dinner.

'Have you tried that yet, love?' Anthony asks Carolyn, pointing to the plate in her hand.

'Nah, I'm starving though. We're gonna eat upstairs if that's okay? This is Thais, by the way,' Carolyn says, pronouncing her name lazily over the i so it sounds more like Tace. 'She's on the Brazilian team. Thais, this is Anthony and Ellen, Jaspa's mum and dad, and her boyfriend, Cooper.'

'No problem, *minha casa e sua casa*,' Anthony says, clearly proud of his Portuguese.

'*Muito bom*, Anthony, very good,' Thais responds. 'Welcome to Brazil.'

'Okay, let's go, I'm starved.' Carolyn leads Thais upstairs and they sit on the two-seater setting on the balcony.

'This is *picanha*,' Thais says, pricking a toothpick into a strip of meat on her plate. 'Then you rub it into the cassava.'

'What's cassava?' Carolyn asks. 'It looks like breadcrumbs.'

'Here, try,' Thais says, bringing the toothpick up to Carolyn's lips and encouraging her to bite into the coated meat. 'Cassava is a vegetable, we eat it many ways in Brazil. Delicious, *sim*?'

'Hell yeah, that's ridiculously yum. I guess I have to delay the notion of ditching meat for a bit longer.'

'You want to go vegetarian?' Thais says. 'I think the world will eventually all need to be, but Brazilian barbecue is so hard for resist.'

'Well, how about we make a pact: we'll go mainly meat-free, but sometimes we can have piconi, picrana … what's it called?'

'*Picanha*,' Thais laughs. 'Yes, I agree. Should we do *promessa de dedo mindinho*? she asks, holding up her pinkie finger.

'*Sim*,' Carolyn says in a thick Australian accent, linking her little finger with Thais'.

'And let's promise to be, how you Aussies say, mates, forever?'

'*Sim*,' Carolyn repeats, with a stirring feeling that completely blindsides her.

#21

Carolyn's pinkie remains entwined with Thais' for a time that lapses long past her comfort threshold for physical touch. Feeling a mix of warmth and confusion, Carolyn drops her gaze. 'You can let go now if you want,' she whispers.

'I don't want. Not just yet.'

Carolyn changes the subject. 'Oh, wow, look.' Beyond the bushes they see the moon creeping towards the sky in a perfect sphere that beams a white light across the ocean.

'*A lua*, must be full tonight. So beautiful. You're so beautiful.'

'What? No, I'm not,' Carolyn says, trying to pull her hand away. 'I'm not stupid, I know I'm not beautiful.'

'Well, I can only know what I know, and I think you're beautiful,' Thais says, curling her remaining four fingers around Carolyn's hand.

The moon appears in full view, intensifying the moment. *Jesus*, Carolyn thinks. *What the heck is going on?* Despite the cool air trickling through the rails of the balcony, Carolyn's skin is clammy. She wants to break apart this situation for fear of where it's leading, but she's also curious to see where it takes her. This doesn't feel normal – at least, it's not what she's used to – but it doesn't feel terrible, either. But it should feel terrible, shouldn't it?

'Carolyn,' Thais says, attempting to soften her matter-of-fact tone. 'I like how you are humble and you have had to fight for things. And you think deeply, even if other people cannot see you are. I can see.'

Carolyn stiffens and she grits her teeth behind her lips. But as Thais brings up her other hand and strokes it softly against the back of Carolyn's neck, she closes her eyes and melts into the moment. It's like when she's paddled furiously against a southerly sweep only to finally relax and allow it to carry her down the beach.

'What's happening here?' Carolyn whispers, her eyes still closed. 'Dude, what's happ–'

'Don't call me dude,' Thais says with soft humour

before leaning into Carolyn so her lips lightly touch Carolyn's cheek.

The inside of Carolyn's mouth tingles, like she's swallowed a spoonful of popping gum. Thais guides the back of Carolyn's head so their lips finally meet, hovering and then touching in a moment of stillness. Carolyn has never experienced such softness before, gentle and caring. Thais' fingers brush the side of her face and she's lost in dizziness as their mouths move into a proper kiss. *She's kissing Thais. Another girl. What does this mean?*

Carolyn's mind bullies into the moment. She jerks back and leans her hand into Thais' shoulder to keep them apart. 'You'd better go,' she says coldly.

Thais wrinkles her brow. 'No, I don't want to go. There is nothing to be ashamed of, Carolyn.'

'Look, I'm not gay, okay?' Carolyn says through clenched teeth in case anyone downstairs is within earshot. 'Please leave.'

'I'm not a label either,' Thais says, attempting to hold Carolyn's hand as she whips it away, out of reach. 'I just feel what I feel.'

Voices can be heard coming through the front door. 'Just go. I don't want you here.'

'Okay, okay,' Thais says, dropping any further

attempts of affection. 'I go. But I am not sorry for this. I wish you luck in the finals tomorrow, *boa noite.*'

'You too,' Carolyn mumbles as she watches Thais walk out of the room. She stands and stares at the door for a moment, a million thoughts buzzing around her head. Mel and Jaspa's voices grow louder as they walk upstairs, so Carolyn takes off her shorts and sneaks into bed without brushing her teeth. She can't tell them about what just happened, it'll ruin everything. Her mind flips through the evening like a series of movie scenes. Each time she gets to the part where she's on the balcony with Thais, the inside of her stomach does somersaults. She mentally replays the moment over and over.

Mel and Jaspa's footsteps draw closer, so she sinks further under the sheet and shuts her eyes, waiting as the laughter grows louder.

'Carolyn, where art thou?' Mel sings as she enters the room, which is only lit with a side lamp.

'Shh, she's already asleep,' Jaspa says as she quietly fishes under the pillow for her pyjamas.

'I'm not so sure, I can see right through that fake breath work.' Mel sits on Carolyn's bed, places a hand on her shoulder and rocks her back and forth. 'Carolyn, you can't go to bed before our daily debrief,' Mel says.

Every night whenever they're on tour, the three of

them lie in their beds and talk about their day, and work through their challenges and worries.

'Don't make me wet willy you,' Mel threatens, licking her finger and hovering it next to Carolyn's ear.

'Alright already,' Carolyn mumbles through the sheet, then throws it back irritably. 'Let's do this. Then I need sleep. I've got the finals tomorrow, in case you'd forgotten.' Carolyn actually had forgotten, after all that's happened in the last two hours to distract her.

Mel and Jaspa brush their teeth and slip into their beds.

'Wow, look at that moon,' Jaspa says as it beams light through their sheer curtains. 'It's so powerful. I wonder if it's going to cause anything cray-cray to happen.'

'What, like hooking up with a Brazilian at the house while your mum and dad are just outside?' Mel says with a giggle.

Carolyn's blood turns cold. How did Mel know? Was she watching from the bushes? She stays silent, not even allowing a trickle of breath to escape.

'What? You did not! Where?' Jaspa says, leaning up on her forearm.

Mel grins. 'In the back laundry.'

Carolyn breathes again. Mel's talking about herself.

'And he is one fine kisser, let me tell ya. So passionate,

like cupping his hands around my face, whispering in my ear about how beautiful I am. He even licked my neck!'

'Eww!' Jaspa loudly says, then claps a hand over her mouth.

'Not eww, it was totally hot.'

Carolyn remains silent, trying not to think about how closely the story parallels her own – minus the neck licking, thankfully.

'What about you, Carolyn?' Mel says.

There's a notable silence. 'What about me what?'

'You totally ripped today, and you've reached the semi finals. That's huge.'

'I really struggled to surf out there today,' Jaspa adds. 'It was really shifty.'

'Yeah, it had these weird rips,' Carolyn says, thankful they've moved on to a subject she's comfortable with. 'I guess I just got lucky.'

'No luck, *chica*, just total skill,' Mel says. 'But, actually, who was the dude on the beach waving you over to that left?' Mel says, unaware of the nerve she's hit.

Carolyn grimaces in the dark. Her body feels so bundled up with secrets, she can barely move. She hates the thought of burdening her friends. But the thump in her sternum is telling her that something's gotta give. It's fine to keep her financial stress from them, and the daily challenges with her mum, and the alcohol-fuelled arguments that echo through her apartment block most nights. But how many more secrets can she carry before she collapses under the weight?

'Umm, well, he's–'

'What, what's wrong?' Mel cuts in.

'Let me finish. I think I've got a stalker,' she blurts, like yanking off a bandaid.

'What?' Jaspa squeals, sitting up straight.

'You what?' Mel repeats.

Carolyn sighs. She doesn't want them to make a big deal about this. 'Since Rio, I've caught this dude staring at me a few times and then he turns up on the beach. It's freakin' weird.'

'We've gotta tell Mum and Dad,' Jaspa says urgently.

'No, no way.'

'But why, Carolyn? They'll help.'

'I said no. I'll deal with it. We're bailing home soon anyway.'

'It's pretty hectic,' Mel says. 'You've gotta promise to let us know if things get too freaky.'

'Okay, I promise. And don't worry, it's not the first time I've had a weirdo in my life. You've met Mum's boyfriends before, so you know.'

'Yeah, but they never stalked you. This is next level. At least let me and Jazz suss out who he is, okay?'

'I dunno, I don't wanna drag you into this.'

'That may be so, but you know we'll do it anyway, so consider us dragged.'

Carolyn sighs. Her heart bangs against her chest. Opening up about this stuff is as exhausting to her as running a marathon would be. She must admit, though, her friends' support is welcome.

Carolyn nods in the moonlit darkness. 'Okay, yeah,' she says. 'That'd be great, thanks.' Revealing one secret makes her feel much better about the even bigger one she's holding onto.

#22

'The key is not being concerned about anyone else's surfing or anyone else's wave. Run your own heat, improve against your own scores.'

Carolyn stands at the water's edge as Thomas coaches her into the second semi final. They've been watching the ocean since 6 am as the junky conditions have progressively grown uglier. Thomas tells Carolyn she should seek out the sets coming in from the north, as they have more potential. She's had butterflies in her stomach all morning, but not because she's one step closer to being a finalist. And not because the surf is so challenging.

She looks out at the line-up to see Thais catch another ride. She's had a brilliant read on the waves that are presenting themselves, and it seems likely that she'll progress from this semi final. If Carolyn makes it through this heat, she'll meet Thais in the final. That's a tough position to be in when you don't want to be within talking distance of someone. As much as Carolyn is drawn to Thais, she can't allow this to happen. She doesn't need this confusing obstacle in her life right now. *She kissed a girl.* When she says it to herself it sounds weird, but when she thinks about the actual moment, it feels perfectly right.

The yellow flag is raised and Carolyn and her three opponents enter the water for their five-minute paddle-out period. With the ocean pushing and pulling in all different directions, they'll need every minute.

'Remember, move fast into your first turn, the waves are short,' Carolyn hears Thomas scream over the sound of the ocean.

On each duckdive, she uses her entire bodyweight, driving her knee into the deck of her surfboard to travel as far under the turbulent whitewater as possible before being catapulted up to the surface on a pocket of air. It takes longer than expected to reach the ideal spot in the line-up. The siren to mark the beginning of her heat sounded eight minutes ago. She looks around to see her opponents also taking a moment to straddle their boards and catch their breath.

Throughout the semi final, Carolyn doesn't feel

particularly skilled, she just feels lucky. The waves that do storm her way provide some opportunity for manoeuvres, but she's not performing anything spectacular. She attempts an air on her fourth ride, but is bucked off by backwash. But as much as she struggles, she still has superior wave opportunity to the other three competitors, who get swallowed up by closeouts or thrown over the falls by waves that bottom out.

In the final two minutes, Carolyn's instinct draws her to paddle into a ball of whitewater. It picks her up and steamrolls behind her as she bounces along the surface until the foam peters out and sucks her into a double-up section. Within moments she's on her feet with her back facing the wave, drawing deep into a bottom turn, then opening up both shoulders to guide her vertically into the top pocket of water. She freefalls hard, meeting the power of the wave on her landing, then flicks her board from underneath her and rolls with the turbulence all the way to shore.

The commentator announces that Carolyn is through to the final. Instead of joy, she feels relief and validation. She wasn't only surfing to meet her own expectations, but also those of the people who helped with her scholarship and fundraising. Emotion chokes her. Wetness forms in her eyes. It's like all her feelings are heightened here in Brazil. She feels an unexpected connection to the country, which doesn't make sense because before this trip, she knew zilch about it.

She spots Mel and Carolyn running down from the competition area, so she uses the bottom of her rash vest to wipe her face, then sucks in a deep breath as they approach.

'You little ripper, you got through!' Mel says, running at full speed and grabbing Carolyn around the shoulders to slow herself down.

'See what can happen when you believe in yourself?' Jaspa says, leaning over to hug Carolyn.

'It was fully tricky out there,' Carolyn says, coaxing them to walk back up the beach so she can get a drink of water. 'How did the other girls go?'

'Everyone struggled a bit. They just chose the wrong waves,' Mel says.

'Which is easy to say from the sand,' Jaspa adds.

'Thais had the same situation in the first semi; all the right rides came to her and not the others.'

Carolyn's stomach ripples like a wave at the sound of Thais' name. She can't figure out if she's angry, sad or excited about what happened last night. Not that it can happen again. There's no chance. The last thing she needs is to give people another reason to think she's a weirdo.

Something up ahead makes Carolyn stop short. 'Hey, isn't that the creep talking to Mr Sampson?'

'Yes, that's what we came down to tell you. We have crucial intel,' Mel says.

'Dude, don't hold out on me, spill it.'

'His name is Noah Machado and he's the founder of a Brazilian surfwear company.'

'Okay, but what's with all the stalky staring?' Carolyn says, handing her board to Mel to give her arm a rest.

'That's what we're not sure about yet,' Jaspa says. 'Maybe it's because of your incredible surfing.'

'But he hadn't seen me surf in Rio.'

'I was wondering the same thing,' Mel says as they walk towards the Australian team tent. 'But he also runs a national program to get girls into surfing. Maybe he's heard about The Bikini Collective and wants to team up.'

'Okay, but why target me? Why not you two as well?' Carolyn says.

Jaspa squints. 'I'm sorry, we haven't got any more answers just yet. But don't worry about it until after the final, okay?'

Carolyn tightens her lips and nods. 'Yeah, you're right. I'm a total scatterbrain at the moment. How long do I have before the final?'

'About forty,' Mel says, putting Carolyn's board on the sand and covering it in a new coat of wax. 'They're running the guys' semis now.'

Carolyn grabs her water bottle and an apple from her bag. 'I'll be back.' The onshore wind whips against her vest as she leaves the tent. She wraps her towel around her shoulders and sits alone on the sand, looking out to sea. The ocean is an unpredictable mess; Carolyn can relate. She starts to dive even deeper into her thoughts. Waves all over the world can be so different – heck, even the difference between Pacific Grove and Bonita Shores is enormous. But they're all considered waves, and surfers can relate to them all in different ways. Perhaps she needs to start viewing *herself* from another perspective and stop trying to fit into moulds that simply aren't made for her.

#23

'Finalists in the water, you have thirty minutes.'

The siren echoes across the ocean as Carolyn straddles her board and moves up and down with the turbulent swell. The tide has dropped, which made the paddle-out a little easier, and is providing some waves with cleaner walls.

She rolls up the sleeves on her green competition vest to a muscle T-shirt fit, to give her more freedom when paddling. A sense of gratitude floods her that she's made it through to the prize money rounds, that she's reached the final, that she's even in Brazil in the first place. It's difficult to convince herself she deserves to win this final; it feels like she should try to cap her potential to remain just below brilliant.

The sun breaks free from the clouds, its light immediately reflecting onto the water. Carolyn breaths an audible sigh of relief and her shoulders relax. It's much more comforting to be able to see what's below, and for some reason waves appear friendlier when sunlit, as opposed to the eeriness than can come with an overcast day.

The ocean shifts underneath her and she barely needs two strokes to paddle into her opening ride. The lip lifts her up like a fairground ride and pitches her onto the wave, leaving her feet to find their position on the surfboard in mid-air. Keeping a low sense of gravity means she's able to soar straight into a bottom turn the moment she thumps onto the landing. A snake of water carves from her board at the top section of the wave, and she grabs her outside rail to accentuate the turn. She has time for two more pumps of her board before performing a precisely-timed snap into the end section.

The leg-rope tightens around her ankle as her board flips about in the shore break. She pulls it towards her and jumps on, but it feels awkward. She shuffles her hips and chest, adjusting her position for ultimate balance. As she paddles back out, she sees Thais soaring down the line towards her. As Carolyn duckdives under the shut-down section, Thais flicks off the wave to avoid the close-out and skims across the water to land right next to Carolyn.

'Phew, that wave was very closing,' Thais says, paddling just an arm's length away from Carolyn.

'Hmph,' Carolyn grunts. She so desperately wants to be infuriated with Thais. How dare she tempt her into a situation she didn't ask for?

'Are you mad at me?' Thais says over the sound of the ocean as they paddle out, side by side.

'Yes. No. I dunno.' Carolyn lowers her head and attempts to out-paddle Thais. She's bad enough at confronting emotions at any time, let alone in the ocean in the middle of her first world junior event final. Jesus, talk about terrible timing.

'Well, I just want you to know,' Thais says, pausing as they both duckdive under the foam and then pop up in unison. 'I'm not sorry for the kiss. I don't have worry if someone is boy or girl, I do not care. I care for you, and I miss you.'

Carolyn stares straight ahead, creating a meditative rhythm with each stroke as the water ripples through her fingers. Thais breaks away to catch her second ride, leaving Carolyn to not only surf her heat, but to battle through her thoughts. There's a pressure on the left side of her chest as her heart protests. When she thinks about Thais, she's overwhelmed by a feeling of being wrapped in a fleece blanket after a mid-winter surf. Excitement and possibilities flare like a sparkler lit inside of her. With Thais she feels respected, with a genuine connection, far more than she's ever experienced with any of the guys she's been with. Which is all great but, *what the heck now?*

The watch she borrowed from Mel tells her there are eight minutes remaining. The last announcement from the beach had her in third place with only one wave caught. Her mood draws her over to the left-handers. On her forehand she feels there's more opportunity to be diverse with her turns, whereas her backhand is mostly about unleashing aggression on the wave with a series of snaps. Today, she feels like she has the ability to tap into the kind of soulful surfer Jaspa is. To slow down and move with ocean, and really *feel* what the wave is inviting her to do.

She sees the yellow five-minute flag raised from the beach. A line of swell scoops her up and propels her into a smooth take-off on the second wave of the set. The open stretch of water gives her the perspective of a video game, so she mentally programs a variety of manoeuvres to keep the judges interested. Her first turn connects perfectly with the top of the breaking water, which gives her the confidence to drop her shoulders and throw her arms behind her to lean into a layback re-entry. Her speedy recovery sees her drawing out a deep bottom turn before soaring up to the top, where she stomps on her back foot to pop out her fins with a fan of water. She hasn't felt this fluid in a long time; perhaps never. Her style is usually more whippy and aggressive. Now, she's waltzing with the wave, using intuition to work out what to do and when to do it. She can picture what her flow would look like on the video screen; no jerky movements and no wasted moments, just a controlled use of speed.

The ride provides her with a 9.2. The siren sounds and she's announced as finishing in first place, pending the calculation of Thais' final wave, which she caught a second before the hooter sounded. Carolyn waits in the shallows, watching Thais draw lines across her wave. She remains transfixed, mesmerised by Thais' ability to place herself in the most visually appealing positions.

Commentary booms from the speakers, noting the similarities between Carolyn's and Thais' last ride. It will be a difficult decision for the judges. Thais needs an 8.7 to win the final.

Carolyn holds her breath as she watches Thais ride towards her, finishing her wave with a critically-timed launch at the closing lip, a turn so dynamic and technical it could add an extra two points to her score. As if in slow motion, Carolyn stares, wide-eyed, as Thais freefalls, her arms suspended in the air, and lands on the water for what seems like a spectacular finish. But she slips. Despite curling her toes to grip into the wax, Thais' front foot glides along the surface of the board and she's unable to recover, landing with a hard slap against the ocean. Every person watching grimaces.

Thais' runaway surfboard flips through the shore break towards Carolyn. She grabs it and sees the snapped leg-rope, then spots Thais bodysurfing towards her.

'Lost something?' Carolyn asks, pushing Thais' board over the whitewater towards her.

Thais takes long strides through the water to collect it. 'Do you mean this?' she says, holding up her surfboard. 'Or the final?'

'Let's just wait for the score,' Carolyn says as they wade slowly together towards the beach. 'Great last wave. Bummer you slipped.' As the words come out, Carolyn realises she'll be as happy if Thais wins the final as Thais will be if she does. 'I think you should take the prize money no matter what,' she blurts.

'No. Why would I do that?'

Carolyn can sense Thais is genuinely shocked by the suggestion. 'Well, cos, you know, you've lived in a favela … I thought the cash would make you happy.'

Thais stops Carolyn by the arm. 'But I am happy.'

'You are?' Carolyn asks, as the commentator tells the

crowd they're moments away from announcing the final results.

'*Sim*, I am. You know, I think you would also be happy if you focus on yourself, live in your own moment, instead of comparing yourself to your friends or how you think people want you to be.'

Waves continue to crash up to their knees, the shoreline rip running rapidly around their feet. Carolyn pauses, squints at the sunlight and sighs. 'I know.'

'Do you, though? It's okay to be sometimes sad about your mum, about, how you say, your housi?'

'Ha, house-o.'

'*Sim*, house-o. Or about needing money for tour. But remember all these things are shaping your picture, you know?'

Carolyn shakes her head, confused. 'My picture?'

'Your picture, like, your story. The *soul* of your story. When you have to fight hard for things, it teaches gratitude, and gratitude helps attract more greatness.'

'Thanks for your patience, folks. We have the final scores.' The commentator pauses. 'Thais, your final ride scored an 8.5. That means Carolyn Fitzgerald from Australia, congratulations, you are today's champion.'

A roar of screams and yelps can be heard from the Australian team. Carolyn drops her board and covers her face with both hands to mask the tears. She feels Thais' arms embrace her, drawing her in close.

'I am so happy for you,' she whispers. 'You deserve this. Enjoy this moment and make it count.'

Carolyn feels Thais' lips brush against her ear, for no one else to see. The whole side of her face tingles, and sensation completely overwhelms her. Perhaps this is also to be a part of her story, a very important part.

#24

Carolyn laughs as Anthony and Thomas crouch either side of her, place her on their shoulders and then rise to carry her up the beach with Mel, Jaspa and the rest of the team surrounding them. She glances back to see Thais' team wrap her in a Brazilian flag. They exchange a smile.

As Carolyn is placed on the ground near the competitors' area, Mel and Jaspa launch over to pull her into a group hug.

'You've won a final, ninja! This is freakin' huge!' Mel says, fighting back the tears.

'You surfed so beautifully,' Jaspa says, handing Carolyn her towel. 'It's like you've been here a million times before, not just a few days.'

'Dudes, I'm freaking out, it's all a bit of a blur. What

do I do now?'

'The guys' final is on, and then there'll be the presso,' Mel says.

'Oh yeah, how did Vijay go, is he in the final?'

Jaspa hands Carolyn a muesli bar. 'Yep, both him and Wil got through.'

'Yew, go the Aussies,' Carolyn says, hoeing into the peanuts and dried fruit. 'Oh crap,' she says, gulping down a mouthful that's bigger than expected. 'Is that the Noah dude talking to Mr Sampson over there?'

They look towards the judging area to see Thomas in deep conversation with a man wearing a black cap, thick-rimmed sunglasses and a T-shirt with the word 'soulfeed' printed on the back of it.

Mel draws in an excited breath. 'Yes, I reckon that's him. That's the name of his surfwear company. Let's go over there.'

Carolyn stiffens. 'No, you reckon we should?'

'Absolutely. Then we can see how he acts with Thommo around,' Mel says, tugging at Carolyn's arm. 'Carn, let's do it.'

Carolyn relents and allows herself to be led by Mel. She grabs Jaspa's wrist. 'You've gotta come too, Jaspa. I can't do this without you.'

As they draw near, Carolyn's heartbeat quickens. She so badly wants to turn around and forget about this mission. Even if this dude's not a stalker, she's still not comfortable with him taking an interest in her. What's so special about her?

'Hello, girls,' Thomas says as they approach. Carolyn takes advantage of Jaspa's height and hovers behind her, slightly out of sight. 'This is Noah. Noah, this is Mel, Jaspa and, hiding behind Jaspa there, our finals winner, Carolyn.'

'*Olá*, congratulations, I saw you surf very well.' He takes off his glasses with a grin. 'How are you enjoying Brazil?'

Carolyn allows Mel and Jaspa to speak as she studies Noah's face, his familiarity once again baffling her. He makes no mention of sponsoring Carolyn, nor The Bikini Collective. So, what's the deal?

'Noah and I met on my first trip to Brazil in 2010,' Thomas says, placing a hand on Noah's back. 'He saved me from being beaten up by some locals.' They both laugh. 'And he has played an enormous role in helping our team for this event, getting our hotels, our transport. We'd be lost without him.'

'Oh, cool,' Mel says, thinking about what questions she can ask to get more information. 'So, have you heard of The Bikini Collective?'

He shakes his head. 'I haven't. What is this, a swimwear company?'

'Oh, nah, it's this group we all started to support girls' surfing. You know, so they all feel connected.'

'The girls have been doing amazing work with this initiative, we're very proud,' Thomas says with a wide grin.

'We wanted to run a surf day while here in Brazil, but Mr Sampson said we had to concentrate on the competition, as we only have a week here,' Jaspa says.

'Do you know much about Australian surfers?' Mel asks, hoping that if he's interested in sponsoring Carolyn, he might include her, too.

'Not much. I know Trudy Hardwick–'

Mel jumps in. 'Yes, she ran a Bikini Collective day with us in Malibu!'

'Yes, and I know you had the incredible Penny Menthol, and now Carolyn Fitzgerald.'

Carolyn feels her cheeks burn, and is struck by a sudden urge to join the conversation. 'Have you been to Australia?' she asks, unsure why she chose that question.

'Yes, but not for a long time.' Noah holds Carolyn's gaze. 'I used to live there, about thirteen years ago.'

He's looking intently at her, the same way he did the other times, but softer now that she can see him in close proximity. The sense of familiarity intensifies. 'Where'd you live?' She's shocked by what she's fishing for. Surely it can't be?

'On the north coast, Pacific Grove,' he says.

In an instant, Carolyn's blood fills with floating ice cubes. She stares into his darkened eyes, eyes she's certain she's looked into before. Her breath shortens as she tries to grapple for words. There's an awkward silence around her. Thomas, Mel and Jaspa haven't caught onto the unravelling conversation.

'Wait a minute, you're ... you're ...' Carolyn chokes on the words.

Noah crinkles his brow, neither confirming nor denying.

Carolyn drops her head and shakes it before breaking away without offering an explanation. She walks to the tent, picks up her bag and starts to run towards the bush track.

'Carolyn! Carolyn!' she hears behind her as Mel and Jaspa sprint up the beach.

'Hey, wait!' Mel grabs onto Carolyn's top and pulls her to a stop, then steps in front of her. 'Jesus, what's wrong?'

Carolyn avoids their eyes. One moment of connection is all it'll take for more than a decade of emotion to come flooding out. Her body stiffens and the doubt starts to creep in. Perhaps she's jumped to a completely ridiculous conclusion.

'This is going to sound totally nuts, but–' Carolyn is

suddenly cut off by a voice behind her.

'Carolyn, please can I talk to you?' Noah says through shortened breath, reaching out to touch her arm. 'Please, can we speak alone for a minute?'

Carolyn yanks her arm away from him. 'If we talk, then it's in front of these guys. They're like my family, which is handy, considering mine ran away from me,' she scolds, holding his stare.

Mel and Jaspa remain silent.

Carolyn folds her arms. 'Okay, you have our attention. Go on, say it. Are you him?' She pauses and then raises her voice. 'I said. Are. You. Him?'

'*Who?*' Mel mouths to Jaspa.

Jaspa shrugs.

Noah squeezes the bridge of his nose, and slowly nods his head. 'I had a daughter in Australia. I haven't seen her for thirteen years.'

Carolyn tightens her lips. 'Just say it.'

He sighs. 'I had to leave Australia. I'd overstayed my visa. Your mother was very protective of you, and we were both so young. I was not ready.' He forms a prayer signal with both hands. 'Please, please, I hope you understand.'

'No freakin' way,' Mel gasps. 'You mean he's your–'

'Yep. He's my dad.'

#25

Carolyn thrusts out her hand towards Jaspa. 'Do you have your phone?'

Jaspa nods and pulls it from her back pocket. 'Hey, are you okay? We're here for yo–'

'Yep,' Carolyn offers shortly. She can't believe this is happening. She can't believe she's about to make this phone call. Years of denial and diversion has led to this moment. 'I'm gonna use it, that okay?'

'Yeah, of course babe, of course.' Jaspa stares back at Mel with a helpless expression.

Carolyn walks away with purpose as Mel and Jaspa remain fixed in place and Noah wanders away holding his head. She dials a number while the commentators lead into the last fifteen minutes of the men's final.

The phone rings out.

She presses redial.

It rings out again.

She presses redial again.

It's picked up after six rings.

'Hello?' says the sleepy voice.

'Mum.'

'Carolyn? It's late here. Is everything okay?'

'No, Tanya. No, it's not. When exactly were you planning to tell me–'

'What's wrong, are you in trouble? Are Anthony and Ellen there?'

'Please, just shut up. There's a weird delay on the phone. Stop talking for a minute and listen. When were you going to tell me about my father, huh? Did you know he lives here in Brazil? Did you know he was going to contact me here? Jesus, Mum, this is freakin' off the hook.' The words get choked in her throat. She blinks back the tears.

After a long pause, her mum finally speaks. 'Oh. So, Noah contacted you?'

'Oh what, *now* you know his name. *Jesus.* Yes, he contacted me. How long since he's contacted *you* is what I wanna know.'

Carolyn hears her mum sniff.

'You must understand, I did it for you. I didn't want him giving you false promises or hope. I had to see that he could prove himself if he was going to be back in your life.'

'How long, Mum?'

There's a deep sigh from the other end. 'He contacted me about four years ago, when you started to get more serious with surfing. And then again recently for the donation.'

'Hold up, the *what*?'

'The donation, the cheque you received. Noah knew you were struggli–'

'*We're* struggling, Mum. We are. Together.'

'Sorry, yes, okay *we*. He asked how he could help, but I said it had to be anonymous.'

'Well, it ain't so anonymous now, is it? Did you know he was gonna stalk me here?'

'He contacted me a couple of days ago and asked if I minded. I said I would get back to him. I really wasn't sure if it was the right thing to do. But it seems he did it anyway. So here we are.'

'So here we are. *Crap.*'

A momentary silence falls as Carolyn scrolls through her thoughts.

'Mum, hang on, he told me he hadn't seen his daughter, me, for thirteen years. But you told me he split the moment I was born. And then there's that photo. What the absolute heck?'

'I just thought it was an easier story to swallow. It's all so complicated.'

'Well, how about you un-complicate it and give me some truths.'

'Noah and I stayed together for just under two years, but we were so young. I didn't see him as a capable father, and he had visa issues. I didn't want a distant parent constantly letting you down. I'm already guilty of that myself.'

Carolyn pauses, reflecting on all the times she's wished her mother would be different, be better, and then sighs. 'No you're not. I know you be the best you can be. Mum. Mum, don't cry. It's okay, we'll work it out. Please don't cry. This might be a good thing. He actually seems pretty cool, and Mr Sampson likes him a lot. He also helped me win one of my heats. Oh, yeah, I won the comp, Mum! I won the whole freakin' comp!'

'Really?' Her mum squeals. 'You won? Carolyn, that is amazing. I'm so proud of you.'

Carolyn holds the phone away from her ear. It's the first time her mum has ever said she's proud of her. 'You are? Thanks, Mum.'

'You know, I've had a bit of a win too. I haven't had a drink or a cigarette in eight whole days.'

'Mum, that's sick!' Carolyn relaxes and allows the tears to fall freely down her cheeks. There's no hope of suppressing them now, there are too many that have gone un-spilt for so long, now scrambling over each other for a release at last.

'Mum,' Carolyn says through the sobs. 'I'd better go, the presentation is soon.'

'Okay, I'll see you when you get back in a few days. You know I love you?'

'Yeah, I know it. I do too. Bye.'

Carolyn hangs up and stares at the ground, taking a moment to collect her emotions. She's got a dad. An actual, real, living father who seems to care about her. So, what does this mean now? What will occupy the space that's been taken up by all that wondering?

She pulls up the bottom of her rash vest, realising she forgot to return it, and wipes the wetness from her cheeks. Mel and Jaspa start to walk slowly towards her, so she makes her way down to meet them.

'I just spoke to Mum,' Carolyn says, handing the phone back to Jaspa. 'God, it's all so intense.'

'Is she doing okay?' Jaspa asks.

'Yeah, I guess. It's probably hard for her, but she seems okay. Relieved, I reckon.'

They look up as the siren sounds, signalling the end of the junior men's final.

'C'mon, let's go – if you're up to it?' Mel says,

swooping an arm around Carolyn's shoulders. 'You've got a podium to get up on.'

A wall of people several rows deep surrounds the beach stage, the finals day drawing a lot of local interest. Carolyn's head is a muddle. There's so much she's had to take in over the last couple of days, she doesn't know whether to feel stressed, or excited, or maddened. Probably all three. Her eyes sting and her head is dizzy from crying, and she can't work out how to get past all of these people.

She picks at her fingernail while leaning into Mel's ear. 'How do I get to the freakin' stage?' Her breath starts to become shallow, and her shoulders stiffen. 'There are too many people here.'

'It's all good.' Mel guides Carolyn by the shoulders as Jaspa uses her height advantage to clear a path for them. 'We've got you, chick.'

They show the security guard their wristbands and stop at the steps. Samba music pumps through the speakers, creating a mass of noise that merges with roars from the crowd. The energy is high, and Carolyn can barely breathe.

'Can you come with me?' she says to Mel and Jaspa, digging her toes into the sand. 'Please, please, I don't wanna go up there on my own.'

'Oh babe, you know we can't, we weren't in the

final,' Jaspa says.

'Yeah, we'll be booed off,' Mel laughs. 'You'll be fine, this is your moment.'

'I'll take you,' says a voice from behind them.

Carolyn turns to see Thais, and happiness instantly floods her body. In all this chaos and commotion, all she cares about is seeing this person in front of her, the person who gets her more than anyone she knows.

'See, it's all good, now you've got your finals podium buddy,' Mel says.

Carolyn and Thais exchange a glance. They know they're much more than buddies.

She follows Thais up the stairs to the platform and walks past the men's junior finalists to stand with the other two female finalists. Carolyn looks down, realising she still hasn't changed out of her contest vest. Carlos strides onto the stage with a microphone, talking to the crowd in Portuguese, then reverts to English to thank all of the sponsors and recap on the day of surfing. He notes Carolyn's barrel in the semi final as one of this year's junior tour highlights. Carolyn can barely contain her nervous grin. Before this event no one knew her name. This country has offered her so much. She wonders if it's because she's rooted to it by DNA.

Each girl from fourth to second place is awarded a

cheque and a trophy. Thais returns from collecting hers and whispers to Carolyn, 'You're up next. Enjoy.'

On the outside, Carolyn's smiling, but on the inside her heart is trying to burst through her ribcage.

'This year's winner of the Praia do Rosa pro junior is a talented surfer all the way from Australia, and she's definitely someone to watch. Give a big hand for Carolyn Fitzgerald,' Carlos says, waving Carolyn over to join him.

She holds her breath and wipes her damp hands on her boardshorts. The crowd calls out to her in a mix of languages as she shakes Carlos's hand and accepts her trophy and a cheque for US$1,000. All of a sudden, a full year on the world junior tour is looking more achievable.

Carlos shoves the microphone in front of Carolyn's face. She furiously shakes her head in horror, but he refuses to remove the microphone, and practically puts it in her hands.

'Ummm, hi,' she sniffs nervously. 'I'd like to thank all of the sponsors, and Mr and Mrs Ryder for helping me get here.' Then someone in the front row catches her eye, making her pause. Noah stands in the middle of the crowd, unmoved by the people pushing and pulling all around him, his eyes fixated on Carolyn and his face beaming with pride. 'I errr ... I'd also like to thank

Brazil for having me. In the short time I've been here I've found a friend,' she turns around to point at Thais, 'and I also found my dad.' The crowd roars, and she smiles down at Noah before returning to the back of the stage while the male finalists collect their prizes.

'You found your *pai*?' Thais says as they walk down the stairs.

'Oh, yeah. I've got so much to tell ya. It'll seriously take all night,' Carolyn says as they reach the sand.

'I don't mind.' Thais winks. 'The more time I get to spend with you before you go, the better. Would you like that?'

Carolyn feels a rush of excitement. 'Yeah, I'd kinda love that.'

Carolyn sees Noah push through the crowd to greet a woman. He takes her hand, and they turn and head towards her.

'I've gotta go,' she says to Thais. 'I'll see you a bit later. No wigging out this time, I promise.'

'Hi,' Carolyn says as Noah approaches. She hesitates, not knowing how much to say. The woman next to him smiles at her as widely as Noah does. 'I, ummm, I spoke to my mum.'

'I know, she called me straight afterwards.'

'Oh.' Carolyn shifts her weight from foot to foot as a well-known Brazilian song comes on in the background, sending the crowd into a frenzy. 'She told me about the money you sent me. Thanks, it helped heaps.'

'You're welcome. I want you to have opportunities in surfing. You are very talented. And I want to make up for not being there for you.'

'Okay, so now what? Like, I don't want your charity, and I'm not gonna call you dad yet, if that's what you're hoping.'

'I don't have any expectations. I'm just happy to finally meet you again. And,' Noah puts his arm around the woman beside him, 'I would like to introduce you to Andrea, my wife.'

Carolyn's eye is drawn to Andrea's belly, which is clearly baking either a baby or a very big cheese ball.

#26

'Nice to meet you,' Carolyn says, picking at her cuticles, wishing she had the courage to ask if Andrea's bump is Noah's baby.

'So, you've noticed, this?' He finishes the sentence by rubbing Andrea's belly.

'Yeah,' Carolyn laughs. 'It's a little hard not to.'

'Well, this means you're going to have a little half-brother. If you want to, that is,' Noah says, looking at Carolyn with pleading eyes.

'Oh holy crap, a *brother*? Man, I can't believe it.' Carolyn grapples for the right words. She never in a million years imagined that finding her father would lead to gaining a sibling. 'That's kinda cool. That's really kinda cool.'

Noah and Andrea look at each other and smile. 'I'm

working on getting things sorted so I can visit Australia again. Once the baby is born we would love to come and visit,' he says.

'Well, yeah of course, if Mum's okay with it.' Carolyn notes how happy Noah looks. She wishes her mum could find someone nice and start fresh. Perhaps now that she knows who her father is, her mum might find it easier to move on.

'I understand. I want to have respect for your mum, she's been very protective of you, and I am very grateful for that.'

Carolyn looks up to see Mel and Jaspa gesturing that they're going to walk back home. 'I guess I'd better go, it looks like the after-party is happening.'

Noah opens out his arms, but Carolyn cuts him off.

'You know, I'm a bit hot and cold with the whole hugging thing, I'd much rather a high-five. Don't take it personally, I'm just not that amazing with people.'

'Hey, it's your space, you do what you want with it,' Noah says, slapping his hand against Carolyn's. 'Have a great party, and let's stay in touch. Please,' he adds. 'Perhaps we can meet for breakfast tomorrow?'

'Yeah of course, sounds good,' Carolyn says, giving him a genuine smile before waving goodbye.

'Hey dudes,' she says through short breaths, catching up to Mel and Jaspa on the bush track.

'Here she is, finally,' Mel says. 'We know you've just found your dad and everything, but the celebrations are waiting for our arrival.'

'Ha, you don't even know the half of it,' Carolyn says as she double checks her pocket to make sure her prize money cheque hasn't fallen out.

'What do you mean?' Jaspa asks.

'Well,' Carolyn says, picking a leaf from shrub as she passes it. 'Noah's wife is pregnant. I'm going to have a baby half-brother.'

Jaspa squeals so loudly, Carolyn can feel the vibration carry through her ear.

'Sorry,' Jaspa says. 'I'm just so happy for you, and you know how much I love babies.'

'Good, well you can do all of the gross stuff, like nappies and snot, and I'll do the fun stuff like teaching him to skate and surf.'

'This is so rad,' Mel says, releasing Carolyn's board from under her arm and handing it to her. 'You're going to have someone to visit in Brazil.'

Carolyn grins. The mysteries that have been hanging over her all make sense now. But she realises there's one more thing she's kept locked away from Mel and Jaspa. She's not even sure what she's meant to do with these feelings, but she does know she needs to share them with her two best friends.

'Hey, can we stop a sec? I've gotta tell you something.' Carolyn looks down at her feet, jiggling her hand against the side of her leg, struggling to know where to begin.

'Okay, we're listening,' Mel says, standing her board upright in the sand and leaning against it.

'Umm …' Carolyn pauses, the nerves stifling her words.

'Hurry up, you know this is cutting into serious party time,' Mel says.

'Shhh,' Jaspa scolds Mel. 'Carolyn?' she asks, simply, but with such kindness.

'Well, you know that Thais chick?' Carolyn looks up at them from underneath her curls.

'Yeah,' Mel and Jaspa chorus.

'We, umm, well, I didn't know it was gonna happen, and I don't even know if it makes me – you know – but we kinda kissed.'

Mel and Jaspa fall silent, then smile to soften Carolyn's unease.

'Well, that's unexpected,' Mel says with a smirk. 'We just thought she was muzzling in to be your next bestie, but it's obviously much more than that.'

'Nah, you guys will always be my best mates.'

'Thinking about it, you and Thais do have a pretty special connection though,' Jaspa says.

Carolyn bites back a smile. She can tell her cheeks are blazing. 'But I don't like girls,' she blurts.

Mel raises her eyebrows. 'Don't you? Thais is a girl.'

'Yeah, but, I dunno. Don't think this means I'm going to wish we were together,' Carolyn says, pointing a finger back and forth between them.

'Why not? We're totally hot,' Mel laughs, grabbing Carolyn around the shoulder and smacking an over exaggerated kiss on her cheek.

Carolyn recoils and cocks her head in protest. 'You know what I mean. Don't be a smartarse.'

'Carolyn,' Jaspa says, reaching out and squeezing her hand. 'We love you, and we're so grateful that you're in our lives; we hope you realise that. We learn so much from you. We don't care who you're with as long as they treat you the way you deserve to be treated. If you're happy, we're happy.'

'Are you happy?' Mel adds.

For the first time in Carolyn's life, she feels like the universe is on her side. She gives in to the grin and allows it to spread across her face, wider than it ever has. 'Yeah, I am,' she says, nodding. 'I'm really freakin' happy.'

Your surf speak glossary!

a-frame a wave peak that peels both left and right.

backside/backhand riding a wave with your back to the ocean.

backdoor entering a barrel from behind the peak.

backwash when water pushes from the shore back towards a regular breaking wave, causing them to collide.

barrel/tube the hollow part of a breaking wave, which surfers can ride inside of, completely hidden from a shore view.

beach break waves that break over sand.

bottom turn generally the first turn you do, performed at the bottom of the wave.

closeout a wave that shuts down without peeling left or right.

cutback a turn you do on the open face to position yourself back near the critical pocket of the wave.

deck the side of the surfboard you lie down on.

drop the ride when you take off on a wave with the pitching lip.

duckdive pushing your board underneath a breaking a wave so you can pop out the other side.

face the 'green' smooth part of a breaking wave that isn't the whitewater.

floater a manoeuvre that involves gliding over the whitewater, usually so you can reach the open face or finish a ride.

frontside/forehand riding a wave facing the ocean.

glassy/glass-off when there is little to no wind and the ocean is smooth like a mirror.

goofy footer a surfer who stands on a board with their right foot forward. (The same term is also used for skateboarding and snowboarding.)

grommet/grom a young kid who surfs.

Huey the surfing god.

impact zone a spot in the line-up where the waves are breaking with the most power (don't get caught there!).

inside the position that's closest to the breaking pocket of the wave, where you have priority to take off over any other surfer. (The term 'caught on the inside' is also used when you're stuck in the impact zone.)

interference when a competitor drops in or obstructs the path of the surfer who has right of wave. The penalty is usually removal of the interferer's highest score.

kook/gumby a derogatory term used to describe someone who isn't a very good surfer.

layback a forehand manoeuvre where you end a turn by

laying your back close to the water. A very '70s-style move.

left-hander a wave that peels left from the viewpoint of the surfer on the wave.

leg-rope the leash that attaches to your surfboard, which is wrapped around the ankle on your back leg.

line-up a position in the ocean where waves are breaking and the surfers are sitting.

lip the first point of a wave that pitches over. The lip can vary in intensity, from throwing with force to form a barrel, to crumbling along the face.

lull the time between sets when no waves are breaking.

natural footer a surfer who stands on a board with their left foot forward. (The same term is also used for skateboarding and snowboarding.)

offshore wind a wind blowing from the land onto the water, which makes the ocean nice and smooth.

ollie getting air by hopping the front of the board out of the water.

onshore wind a wind blowing from the ocean onto the land, making the ocean bumpy and sometimes tricky to surf.

outside a position that's on the other side of the surfer who's closest to the breaking pocket of the wave. When you're there you have to give way to the inside surfer, unless they encourage you to 'GO!'

out the back the furthest out to sea you can be, on the other side of the breaking whitewater, while still in a position to catch waves.

overhead when you're riding a wave and its face is taller than you are.

over the falls when you take off but don't get to your feet, and fall with the pitching lip. Wipeout!

peak the point of a wave that pitches up, ready to break.

pop-up jumping to your feet on the take-off – the quicker, the better!

pull in what you do when you see a tube/barrel forming before you.

quiver collective noun for surfboards.

rail the edges around the sides of a surfboard, which you ideally want to carve deep into the water on your turns.

reef break a wave that breaks over reef – sometimes dead coral, sometimes alive. Be careful of your feet!

right-hander a wave that peels right from the viewpoint of the surfer on the wave.

roundtail when the tail of a surfboard is rounded – often preferred for barrelling waves.

re-entry (reo) a manoeuvre where you soar vertically into the top pocket of the wave and snap the board around underneath you.

set a group of waves that are usually bigger than the average on the day.

shaper someone who makes surfboards.

soul arch when you're on a wave and you stand stylishly still and tall for a moment with your back arched, old-school style!

squaretail when the tail of a surfboard is squared off at the end.

swallowtail a v-shape cut out of the tail of a surfboard.

take-off the moment you stop paddling for a wave and stand on your surfboard.

wipeout ooops, you've fallen off the wave!

The
Bikini
Collective
Book 1: Ocean Rules
By Kate McMahon

Three friends discover, surfing just got serious

What does it take to be the best, and what does that even *mean* anyway? Fifteen-year-old Jaspa Ryder is on the crest of qualifying to join surfing's prestigious World Junior Tour along with her best friends, Mel and Carolyn. But as the girls soon discover, the ride to stardom doesn't come easy. Jaspa's head and heart are in battle – she isn't sure she *wants* to be a professional surfer, which, given her incredible talent, infuriates everyone, especially her envious brother. Who will qualify for the tour? Will Jaspa's friendships survive the pressure of competition? Sometimes in life, you just have to jump to your feet, take off, and hope you don't wipe out.

"I felt utterly invested in Jaspa, Mel and Carolyn's surfing journey; can we be friends?" **Stephanie Gilmore**

"A book that gets to the heart of surfing friendships and competition. A must-read for all young ocean lovers." **Layne Beachley**

The
Bikini
Collective
Book 2: Lost in LA
by Kate McMahon

Pack your bags, the Bikini Collective girls are California bound to compete in their very first overseas surfing event. The LA sun is shining, Santa Monica's shops are bursting with bargains and the point break is pumping. It should be happy days, right? Wrong! Mel has her party pants on and is ready to ravage this Hollywood scene, but her best friend and wingwoman, Jaspa, is welded to the hip of her new boyfriend. If Jaspa wants to be the Mayor of Lame Town, Mel figures she'll just have to find someone else to get into trouble with. Swept along by the local celebrity brat pack, Mel finds herself on a wild ride that soon lands her in deep water. This is an adventure to rival any rogue set, so hold your breath and dive down deep … and pray you pop back up again!

"A ride so fun and wild, I wanted to stowaway in their surfboard bags." **Laura Enever**

"An exhilarating read that beautifully captures the spirit of being a young professional surfer growing up on tour, and the complicated dynamics of competing against best friends." **Jessi Miley-Dyer**